I0762006

SEE HER HIDE

(A Mia North FBI Suspense Thriller—Book 2)

Rylie Dark

Rylie Dark

Debut author Rylie Dark is author of the SADIE PRICE FBI SUSPENSE THRILLER series, comprising six books (and counting); the MIA NORTH FBI SUSPENSE THRILLER series, comprising three books (and counting); the CARLY SEE FBI SUSPENSE THRILLER, comprising three books (and counting); and the MORGAN STARK FBI SUSPENSE THRILLER, comprising three books (and counting).

An avid reader and lifelong fan of the mystery and thriller genres, Rylie loves to hear from you, so please feel free to visit www.ryliedark.com to learn more and stay in touch.

ISBN: 978-1-0943-9383-4

BOOKS BY RYLIE DARK

SADIE PRICE FBI SUSPENSE THRILLER
ONLY MURDER (Book #1)
ONLY RAGE (Book #2)
ONLY HIS (Book #3)
ONLY ONCE (Book #4)
ONLY SPITE (Book #5)
ONLY MADNESS (Book #6)

MIA NORTH FBI SUSPENSE THRILLER
SEE HER RUN (Book #1)
SEE HER HIDE (Book #2)
SEE HER SCREAM (Book #3)

CARLY SEE FBI SUSPENSE THRILLER
NO WAY OUT (Book #1)
NO WAY BACK (Book #2)
NO WAY HOME (Book #3)

MORGAN STARK FBI SUSPENSE THRILLER
TOO LATE (Book #1)
TOO CLOSE (Book #2)
TOO FAR GONE (Book #3)

CHAPTER ONE

Pushing open an umbrella, Carlina Adams stepped out into the storm.

"One of those stupid Dallas storms," she mumbled under her breath as a cool wind blew raindrops against her cheeks. "All fuss, but they never last long. I bet by the time I get home, it's over."

Their Oak Cliff neighborhood was an established one, with mature trees and sprawling yards. The shortcut between their homes cut through a small forest in the center of the development. As kids, she and Evvie constantly played among those trees. They'd even built a tree-house there, once.

She tilted the umbrella back and tried to see its remains among the dark outlines of the branches, but she quickly realized she could see nothing. Grabbing her phone, she turned on the flashlight to guide her way.

Shining it down on the path in front of her, she saw thick mud.

Great. There go my new sneakers.

She stepped carefully, taking a more roundabout path on higher, less muddy ground. Though she knew each tree here like the back of her hand, now, in the pouring rain, the place seemed eerie, sinister.

Of course, the Marlene Dotts thing had really sent shockwaves through this quiet neighborhood. There was no doubt about that.

Marlene had been a classmate of Carlina's, at Oak Cliff High School in Dallas. Okay, yes, she was a bit of a bitch, but a lot of girls at school were. She was pretty, vivacious. She'd gotten accepted to Stanford. She was going places.

And then, on her way home from school one dark night of March, she'd disappeared.

Her body had been found, not far away, on the outskirts of a safe, family neighborhood like this one. She'd been strangled and dumped there.

That was . . . wow. I guess we're coming up on the one-year anniversary of that, Carlina thought as she pulled her hood tighter around her face.

It almost seemed wrong that here they all were, finishing up their first year of college, when Marlene's life had been cut short. Marlene had been part of her circle of friends, and the murder had certainly thrown everything haywire. The excitement of the last months of senior year and graduation was dampened in a big way. Shocked friends huddled together for weeks in the hallways, crying instead of sharing news of college acceptances. Prom was canceled. Vigils were held. The funeral and memorial service were so well-attended, Carlina hadn't even been able to get in the door.

People had a right to be obsessed with it, though. It wasn't just that Marlene was young and beautiful, cut down in her prime.

No, it was that the killer had never been found.

The surrounding neighborhood was wealthy—they hadn't had a murder in years. And an especially brutal, unsolved murder? No one in their right mind could do such a thing, and so that meant there'd been an insane person in their midst.

Probably a transient. But no one knew for sure. Needless to say, people were still worried about it.

Now that Carlina thought about it, that was probably why her mother had been so concerned about her going out, alone. Even though a whole year had passed, Marlene hadn't been forgotten. There were too many crazies out there.

She moved faster. For the first time, she wished she'd taken the more direct path, sneakers-be-damned.

Thankfully, though, when she took another few steps, the back porch lights of the homes in her development came into view.

She heaved a sigh of relief and ran the last few steps, joining her regular path through the mud, only stopping a couple times, when her umbrella snagged on a branch.

Before long, she arrived at the back fence of her backyard. Slipping around it, she saw the lights of the living room ablaze—her mom was probably home, reading there in her usual spot on the sofa.

She made her way past the old swing set that her father hadn't quite gotten around to removing, and crept around the side of the house to the driveway.

Sure enough, by the time she got there and saw her gray SUV, parked in the C-shaped driveway, the rain had thinned to a light drizzle. She stepped through puddles, searching out the windows of her car.

They were all up. False alarm.

Brilliant, she thought with a roll of the eyes. *What a waste of time. I'm such a ditz. I'd probably trip if a serial killer was after me.*

She turned to her front door, wondering if she should go in and say hi to her mom, but then thought better of it. *If my mom knows I'm here, she'll give me the guilt trip and make me stay in.*

She was just about to turn and head back to Evvie's place when she heard a sound behind her.

She stiffened, thinking of poor Marlene. Out, walking alone, home from soccer practice. Maybe on a night like this . . .

Whirling, she searched the darkness. Her neighborhood was eerily silent. The lights were on all over the streets, making the puddles in the road glisten, but even so, the normally busy neighborhood was quiet. There wasn't another soul around.

It must've been an animal. *We get way too many squirrels around here,* she thought to herself. She'd nearly run two of them over when she returned earlier that day from Tulane.

Making her way to the back of the house, she peered in a window. Sure enough, her mother was curled up under a blanket, reading.

Oh, well, Carlina thought, closing her umbrella. *What she doesn't know won't hurt her, either. And she'll never find out, no matter how much she snoops in my room.*

She turned to head across the lush, wet lawn, toward the woods. The second she stepped that way, though, she heard another sound.

This time, from behind the ancient swing set.

The swing set, with its big wooden clubhouse, had been her refuge as a little girl. Now, it was abandoned, a pile of decaying firewood, ready to become a bonfire. It looked like a small mountain in the darkness, the broken swing hanging askew from the rusted chains. The sound of dripping water all around buffeted her ears as she stepped toward the back fence.

And then the sound came again. It wasn't a cracking branch, though. It sounded more like a scraping, like fingernails raking down a rough piece of bark. This time, she wasn't sure where it'd come from. Behind the swing set?

Maybe there was an animal there, hurt. Once, her father had found a bird's nest that had fallen from a tree. They'd managed to save a couple of the baby birds, but they'd all died over the next few days.

She crept to the edge of the wooden monstrosity and peered around the corner, shining her flashlight this way and that, afraid of what she might see.

But there was nothing. No animal. Nothing but wet grass and a few bushes that lined the back of their property.

Sighing with relief, she turned to make her way into the woods and back to Evvie's. *Brendan already thinks I'm stupid. And he's going to think I'm even stupider when I tell him about the windows.*

She'd just made up her mind not to tell him—there were plenty of things she kept from him, after all—when the figure moved in her periphery.

At first, she thought it was an animal. A large one. But then, suddenly, hands wrapped around her neck, squeezing all the sound from her throat. A warm breath grazed her cheek.

It occurred to her in a rush that she was being strangled. Why? Gasping for air, she tried to form the question, but the pressure on her throat was too much. All the dreams and wishes she'd had, all of her excitement for the future . . .... they all seemed to be fading away, as her lungs began to ache. Hot tears dripped down her cheeks while her mascara melted into her eyes, making them burn as they bulged from their sockets.

The air was quickly leaving her lungs and her entire body started shaking from the fear of what was about to happen. She pounded futilely while her sneakered feet scrabbled for purchase on the muddy ground.

Marlene . . .

The name flitted through her mind. Her vision grew blurry, a sharp pain spreading through her head. Her heart's thudding echoed through her ears, and for a brief moment, she wondered if Marlene's fate would be her own.

No . . .

She had never wished to be able to scream as much as she did in that moment.

But it wasn't possible.

She stared into the void, her last breath leaving her, until her eyes could see no more.

CHAPTER TWO

Mia North sat on a park bench, holding that crumpled sheet of paper, staking out the home of one of the Dallas Fort Worth Police Department's finest—Detective Kevin Reynolds.

Well, finest *is a matter of opinion*, she thought bitterly, pushing away thoughts of Kelsey. Right now, her almost nine-year-old daughter would be getting out of bed.

Which meant that Mia had missed yet another home-cooked breakfast from mom.

All because of this bastard.

She checked the address. Yes. It matched. That's where that jerk lived.

That's where he slept, where he ate, where he enjoyed time with his family . . . while Mia North skulked around, day after day, hoping to avoid getting caught. She could barely take a single breath without worrying someone was on her tail.

Because of him.

Kevin Reynolds.

Well, Wilson Andrews, actually. Wilson Andrews was the senate hopeful who, in effort to protect his insane brother Jerry, had tried to pin a number of his crimes on Mia. She'd been an easy target, since she'd been arrested and convicted for the murder of one Ellis Horvath, who'd been stalking her young daughter Kelsey. All it had taken was Kevin Reynolds to do a little behind-the-scenes evidence-meddling, and she'd come out looking guilty as sin.

Kevin had to have been paid off by Wilson Andrews. She knew it. She knew there was a connection somewhere. There had to be.

She just had to find a way to prove it.

This felt like it. If she could get inside his house, maybe she could find some evidence that tied the detective to the senate hopeful. Maybe she could find out exactly what he was doing, lurking about the warehouse where Ellis Horvath was killed.

Her fingers curled into fists as she sat near the old beater car she'd bought for $200 off a shady lot outside of town, waiting for the man of the hour to make an appearance. He'd have to leave, soon, for work . . . wouldn't he?

But she'd been sitting there, on the park bench across the street from his apartment building, waiting for an hour. No Reynolds.

Screw this, she thought, checking the time on her burner phone. It was almost nine o'clock. Impatient, she tucked the paper into her jacket, pulled the hood up over her dark ponytail, pushed her dark sunglasses up on her nose, and jogged across the street.

The apartment building was a box, with a single, glass door in the center. When she walked past, peering in innocently, she saw a foyer with a few mailboxes. She scanned the area to make sure no one was watching. Then, taking a chance, she climbed the three short steps and tried the door, expecting it to be locked.

But it opened easily.

She stepped inside and strode briskly to the mailboxes. The floor was old linoleum and the dozen or so mailboxes were once-brass, now worn and scratched, with various colored placards containing many names, some faded, some brand new.

Kevin Reynolds's name looked like the newest of them all. She inhaled sharply as she read the number of his apartment: 3E.

E, she thought, *Third floor.*

The stench of cat piss hit her as she turned to climb the crumbling stairs.

Somehow, I get the feeling Kevin Reynolds is not married. No married woman would live in this place. I bet he's newly divorced, she thought. *Good.*

Though it was nowhere near the horrors she'd been through, what with the arrest, the conviction, the weeks in prison . . . it was a little bit of bleakness in his life. She didn't wish ill on anyone, really, but with people like him and Wilson Andrews? It was hard not to.

As she climbed the steps, the stench of cat urine combined with that of old garbage. She held a hand over her nose and continued on.

The caustic scent only seemed to grow as she made her way down the hallway, 3A, 3B, 3C . . .

Suddenly, a door behind her swung open. An older, female voice barked, "What are you? Who are you? You one of them prostitutes? Drug dealers? This is a respectable place! We don't need none of your kind, skulking around here!"

Mia whirled, shaking her head. She found a stout woman with gray, pin-curled hair, brandishing a broom, as if she intended to use it as a weapon on Mia. “No, I’m just . . .I’m from public works. I’m investigating that smell.”

The woman scowled. “What smell? Where’s your credentials? You’re a lying hussy, that’s what you are. We don’t need no more prostitutes around here. Drug users. You people give our place a bad name, coming in here, all shady-like.”

Mia turned and took a step away from the woman, hoping she’d leave her alone.

But she cringed when the woman shrieked, “Hey! You listen to me! I’m calling the police!” and slammed the door to her apartment, making the walls rattle.

The police. She had to get out of here. But as she was about to turn, at around 3D, the horrific smell took on another quality, one that made her eyes water and her heart jam in her throat.

She knew that smell fairly well, because it was distinct and unforgettable. It smelled sickly sweet, like that of a decaying corpse.

She inhaled deeply, to be sure.

Something was definitely wrong up here on the third floor.

She broke into a run, heading for 3E, which happened to be at the end of the hallway. When she got there, she stopped. The stench was stronger than ever. She placed her hand on the doorknob, debating what she should do. She couldn’t knock—what if someone answered?

So she quietly turned the knob. It clicked and gave way.

Mia pushed slightly, and the door opened a crack.

She was hit with a wall of odor so strong, it felt like a physical force, pushing her back. It seemed to get in her pores, pulling tears from her eyes. Gritting her teeth, she nudged the door open a little more.

The apartment was dark. Light-blocking shades had been pulled down tight over two windows beyond an overstuffed couch, so only a small bit of light escaped from their dark outlines.

It was enough to illuminate the shape of the body, sprawled out on the threadbare rug. A black slick of blood seemed to spread from the shape, like a twisted cape.

She held her nose and crept forward until she was nearly over the dead man’s face. His skull had been smashed in, and his face, a Halloween mask of gore and mangled flesh. One eye hung loose from the ocular nerve, resting on a bloated cheek, likely popped from its place by the force of the blow. Maggots wriggled in the open sore.

She scanned the rest of the body, pushing aside his tweed blazer to reveal the badge on his belt. As grotesquely misshapen as the face was, there was no doubt.

This was Kevin Reynolds.

Which meant that her one lead, her one chance of finding justice and clearing her own name . . . was gone.

She hadn't been affected by the stench before, but now, she stifled a gag. Covering her mouth, she reversed direction and fled.

It was only when she reached the door that she heard the sirens.

Hell. Just her luck. That neighbor hadn't thought to call the super about the horrible smell, but she'd found it important enough to call the police about *her*.

She threw open the door to the lobby and found the stout lady, glaring at her and waving a rolled-up magazine at her, like she was a fly she wanted to smack. "I told you! I told you I'd call the police!"

The sirens were getting closer now. After a few weeks on the lam, Mia could tell fairly surely how far away they were by volume. They were probably mere blocks away. Unless she really wanted to go back to prison without clearing her name, she didn't have time to spare.

There was an unmarked door in the hallway, across from her. Rushing ahead, she pushed it open to find a staircase.

The old woman screamed, "You stay here, you hussy! You drug dealer! You let the police come talk to you!" but Mia threw herself down the steps, taking them as fast as she could.

On the ground floor, there were two doors—one with a window, from where she could see the downstairs mailboxes, and another, solid metal door. She pulled that one open carefully and peered out to a small, empty alleyway, backing up to a solid wooden fence. Beyond that, there was a line of trees. She noticed a small hole in the fence. *Could I fit through that?*

She'd have to try.

She slipped out and crouched behind the dumpsters there, peering through the crack between them and the wall as a police car skidded to a stop outside the complex.

Taking a deep breath, she rose from her hiding spot, and, hugging the wall, crept closer to the opening in the fence. When she was directly in front of it, she decided that yes, she would be able to fit into the narrow opening, with inches to spare.

Ducking her head, she slipped through the small space, the top of her hood catching on the splintered wood, but she did not stop. Not until she was out of the woods, in the backyard of a home, and the apartment complex was out of sight.

She dug her hands into her pockets and found the paper with the scrawled address, from her partner, David Hunter. *Thanks, buddy. But it looks like this one's a dead end.*

Had Andrews thought he would snitch, and offed him?

It didn't matter. Kevin Reynolds couldn't help her, now.

Her heart sunk. Her best lead, gone.

Even so, she was sure David Hunter had more leads to give her. Wilson Andrews left a lot of threads dangling in the business he was involved in. She was sure David had the connections she needed to find one of those dangling strings. One she could pull and pull until the whole fabric of his life unraveled and proved the entire case against her a fraud.

David would come through. He was doing what he could, within the confines of his job, trying not to get caught. But she had nothing to lose, and she couldn't simply wait.

No. Her heart lurched at the thought of Kelsey and her husband Aiden, spending another day without her.

She'd have to find a way to get in touch with David and hope he had more dirt on Wilson Andrews to give her.

CHAPTER THREE

David Hunter rubbed the back of his neck, something he always did when he was stressed out.

His son, Louie, was being a brat, complaining about oatmeal for breakfast again. As a single father, the buck should've stopped with him. And yet the kid was getting as bad a mouth as *he'd* once had, at that age.

Seven a.m. phone calls were never a good thing, in his line of business. This one had been from Special Agent in Charge Pembroke—his boss. Something about a murder. A kid. But damned if he could register a single word, with his son, carrying on about the raisins in the bowl looking like dead bugs.

"Hold on," he spoke into the phone. He looked at Louie. "Just . . . deal with it. Pick them out if you have to!"

He started to step out of the kitchen when Louie crossed his arms and pouted, "Screw you, Dad. *You* pick them out."

"Hey. Watch the language. If you want to starve, fine. You're not getting Froot Loops." He motioned to the phone. "I've got to take this. It's important."

He cradled the phone to his ear and hit the foyer as his son screamed, "It's always important, Dad. You care about your job more than you care about me!"

Great. A perfect time for a Louie tantrum. Yet, these days, they seemed to be getting worse and worse, more and more frequent.

Closing the accordion doors as he glared at his son, he took a deep breath and spoke into the phone, "Yeah, I'm here. Sorry about that."

Pembroke was a fair man, but he couldn't be bothered with anything that wasted his time. He grunted. "As I was saying. We have an eighteen-year-old victim who was strangled outside her home in Oak Cliff. Body was found about an hour ago. Her parents found her. One Carlina Adams. The daughter was on break from college, visiting friends, and didn't make it home."

That was interesting. He'd grown up in Oak Cliff. It was full of wealthy, safe neighborhoods. It wasn't exactly a hotbed of crime.

Especially murder. But sad as it was, it was just another murder, and there were plenty of those in Dallas. This wasn't exactly something his unit dealt with. Unless . . . "Why are you calling me?"

"Because it occurred in the same neighborhood as another murder, almost a year ago. An eighteen-year-old girl named Marlene Dotts disappeared walking home at night after soccer practice, and her body was found, strangled, a few blocks away from her house. This victim—a Carlina Adams—was also strangled. She was found in her own backyard. It's possible the two could be related. They attended the same high school—Oak Cliff."

"Oak Cliff High? Shit. I went there," he said, shaking his head. Back when he went to school, the biggest criminal act he knew about was some kids getting suspended for smoking behind the dumpsters. Times sure had changed.

"I said you'd be over to check it out. Address is 23432 Maple Street. The police are on the scene. How fast can you get there?"

"I got to take my kid to the bus stop, but I'll be there. Half hour?"

"All right." His boss hung up without another word, and Hunter got the feeling his boss was disappointed his answer wasn't *immediately*.

But Pembroke was always disappointed. Mia had been his Golden Girl, the one he relied on, the one who could do no wrong. When Mia had something to do with her daughter, he allowed it, no questions asked. Now, without Mia on the force, David had hoped he could have a chance to prove himself. Instead, with Mia gone, Pembroke only seemed to rail on him, harder.

He pulled open the accordion doors to find his son scraping the bowl of oatmeal into the trash. He peered in and found the remains of pretty much the entire helping, in the garbage.

Of course. He let out a sigh and pocketed his wallet and keys. "Don't blame me if you're hungry. Put that stuff in the dishwasher and brush your teeth. On the double. I've got to get you to the bus stop."

Louie's "on the double" was actually slower than his normal snail's crawl. Finally, David had to nudge him along.

"You're going to come to my game today, after school, right?" Louie asked when he'd finally gotten him and his backpack into the car.

Damn. His little league game was today. He was starting first baseman for the Thunder. "I'll try to be there. If not, Mrs. Foster will."

Louie pouted and looked out the window. "So that's a no. Figures."

“Hey. I said I’ll try,” David said, pulling out of his driveway. “That’s the best I can do.”

But with a new case consuming him, he knew what would happen. He’d get wrapped up in it, like he always did. He’d work like hell to prove himself to Pembroke.

And that meant family would do what it always did. Play second fiddle.

Which was exactly why Lorraine had left him, three years ago, not long after he became an agent.

And for Louie, who seemed to resent him more and more every day, David knew his best would never be good enough.

*

David was still thinking about Louie when he got to Maple Street in Oak Cliff.

Actually, he was thinking about Kelsey, Mia’s daughter.

When they were partners, Mia rarely slept. She always had her nose to the ground, sniffing out these cold cases. She was always working. And yet somehow, she’d managed to keep a healthy relationship with her husband. With her daughter.

How the hell had she managed that?

Why had he gotten the short end of the stick? Was it him? Was it bad luck? He couldn’t say he was jealous—he sure as hell wasn’t jealous of what Mia had been going through, lately—but he couldn’t help but feel a little sorry for himself.

Speaking of Mia, he wondered where she was. He checked the news, all the time, expecting to receive word that she’d been apprehended. She couldn’t be out there for long, not with all the surveillance and media attention, all the time.

But she was smart. She knew how to evade them. And she had, for nearly three weeks.

Eventually, though, she’d be in touch with him. That’s what she told him, when he gave her that information he thought would help her along.

Kevin Reynolds. He wasn’t sure what it would bring, but it’d been something, and Mia was hungry for any bit of help.

And he wanted her cleared. He wanted her back on the job. It was his testimony that had probably been the final nail in the coffin that sent her to prison for life. But even from that moment, he'd known Mia North wasn't a killer. He'd believed there had to have been some mistake.

And he knew that eventually, Mia North would figure it out. She was a smart one.

All those thoughts quickly evaporated when he took in the scene before him—half a dozen police cars and several news vans, lining the streets. A reporter stood on the sidewalk, giving a morose account of the crime, as a cameraman filmed. Various people milled about, some in uniform.

David pulled to the side of the road and got out, affixing his badge to his waist. When he got there, he found a couple of the officers he'd worked with in the past. Lieutenant Briggs was calling out orders, so David decided he was the one in charge.

Unfortunately.

Briggs was, in every way, an obstruction. Whereas most of the Dallas Fort Worth Police Department welcomed the help of the FBI, Briggs saw it as an insult. Briggs had been brusque with David, a year ago, when he'd made inquiries into the Marlene Dotts case. And even before that, Mia had told him once that she'd locked horns with him on another big case—the kidnapping of a little girl. The Franklin girl. No matter what Mia had said to be gentle about the fact that they were taking over the case, since it matched a series of cold cases they'd been investigating, Briggs gave her trouble. He refused to cooperate, keeping evidence to himself, generally making things hard. Even so, the FBI had found the kidnapper.

Actually, Mia had. It'd been all her, her dogged determination to find answers that had led her to the man, the girl's uncle.

Of course, when Mia did find him, Briggs had taken all the credit.

That guy's nothing but a big snot, Mia had said about him, afterwards. But that was it. She wasn't much for the glory and the accolades. She wanted the job done, right, and as quickly as possible.

He found himself smiling at that as he jogged across the street to meet the lieutenant. The man was over six-five, and his body was a brick wall—not fit and lean and muscular, like David's form, but solid. His men followed as he barked orders and pointed fingers, eagerly lapping at his heels like his trained lackeys, because just by sight, he wasn't a man you'd want to have on your bad side.

Unfortunately, David Hunter was already there.

That much was evident when Briggs took one look at him and rolled his eyes, then rubbed his square, meaty, linebacker's jaw. "Oh, great. You?" he barked.

David nodded. "Me."

"Well, what a great day it is for me. Why are you here, Hunter?"

"Because you might remember the Marlene Dotts case, last year? This one is supposedly pretty similar."

Briggs rolled his eyes. "Of course, I remember it. I worked on it."

"Then you should remember that it went unsolved." Hunter couldn't help but take great pleasure in reminding him of the fact. "And the case went cold. You're not actively pursuing leads, I'm assuming."

"Yeah," he muttered something under his breath and motioned for him to follow. "All right. Fine. Let me show you what I've got. They're taking evidence right now. Haven't moved the body. You got here while it's still warm."

Hunter followed him down a pathway of circular stones, around the back of a charming ranch house. "What have you seen so far? Any determinations?"

"A few. I'll let you make your own conclusions."

Of course. The man didn't like to share.

The backyard was shaded with mature trees, and there was an old, rust-and-decayed-wood swing set, in the process of being engulfed by the surrounding vegetation. As they traversed the patio and came to the edge, Hunter noticed a number of officers, gathered around a spot in the corner of the yard, near an old shed. Two men crouched there, one taking photographs.

Steeling himself, he walked the rest of the way.

The girl was pretty. It was easy to tell that, even in her condition. She had long hair that still managed to look blonde, despite being crusted with dirt and dried leaves. It curled down past her shoulders, almost to her waist. Her limbs were long and well-shaped, though now they bore the pallor of death. She was lying in an almost fetal position, her jacket and sweatshirt pulled up to reveal a swath of pale belly. She was missing a single sneaker, and her delicate toenails were painted a light pink.

H sucked in a breath. He didn't have daughters, but anytime a young girl like this was found, it tugged at the heartstrings. "She was found just like this?"

Briggs nodded. "They haven't moved her."

Hunter's eyes caught on the red marks, around her throat. Looked like a cord. "So not manual strangulation?" he said aloud.

"Uh-huh," Briggs said.

"We have a ligature?"

"Nope. Whatever they used, looks like some kind of cord. But it was missing."

"Got her from behind, hey?" He craned his neck to get a better look. "So it's possible it could've been a stranger who surprised her."

"Yep," Briggs remarked, clearly determined to be as unhelpful as possible.

A passing officer heard his conjecture and added, "Or it could've been one of her friends. That's where she was, visiting with friends. Over there." He pointed through the woods. "Supposedly she left alone for a few minutes, and was supposed to come back, and she never did. Her friend got worried when she didn't return and called her mom."

Finally, someone was helpful.

It was short-lived. Briggs glared at the kid, who scurried off, tail between his legs.

"Any idea as to where it happened?" Hunter asked.

Briggs motioned him over to another part of the yard. It was muddy from the recent rainfall, and there were a number of footprints on the ground, of all sizes. The prints seemed to trail a muddy path through the woods. He could just make out the other houses through the trees. "Probably right around here. No sign she was dragged anywhere."

"So someone was waiting in her backyard to kill her," Hunter said, tapping his chin. "Did anyone interview possible witnesses? Anyone see anything?"

"We're still piecing it together, talking to neighbors. You're welcome to. Mrs. Adams is a basket case, but Mr. Adams is inside. Guess you could probably talk to him."

Guess I will, Hunter thought, happy to leave him behind. He took a few steps forward and then stopped. "Lieutenant, I'm going to look into this a little more, but if we find out that there's sufficient evidence to tie this case to Marlene's? We're going to be working alongside you." *And that means taking it over from you completely and using your men at our will. Tough.*

Briggs frowned. The bastard had the audacity to turn away without a response.

Hunter walked up the slate patio, past a giant outdoor grill and dining table, and climbed a couple steps to the back door. He stepped inside and found a tall man in a rumpled suit, leaning against a kitchen counter, holding a coffee cup at chest level, staring solemnly at nothing. A silver nameplate on his breast said, *Copeland Adams.*

"Mr. Adams?" he asked.

The man turned, "Yes?"

"I'm David Hunter. FBI. I'm investigating the death of your daughter. Let me first start off by saying that I'm very sorry for your loss, and realize this is a terrible shock to you."

He nodded absently.

"I wonder if I can ask you a few questions?"

"Of course," he motioned for David to sit at a tile-topped dining table.

David sat across from him and pulled out a pad and pen. "I understand you weren't home when this happened, and your wife called you? Where were you when you heard about your daughter?"

"I was working. I work as an overnight auditor at the Royal Embassy Hotel in downtown Dallas. My wife called me at one to tell me that she was worried, because Carlina hadn't come home. I told her not to worry, because they were all watching movies. Then she called me again to tell me that she'd heard from her best friend, Evelyn Rhinehart, and that she wasn't there, and in fact she'd left at a little after ten, promising to be back, but she'd never returned." He sighed, "I decided I'd come home right away. I did at around two and we started looking for her."

David scribbled down the name Evelyn Rhinehart. "And what happened then?"

"We went looking for her. All of us. Evelyn and her boyfriend and I guess some guy Carlina was seeing. There's a path behind the house that they always used to take as a short-cut. You saw it back there?"

He nodded.

"Well, we walked that path, again and again. Nothing. It was only when the sun started to come up, and one of us looked behind the swing set, that . . ." His head hung low. He paused, composing himself, and rubbed his eyes with one hand, dragging it down his face. "That was when we found her behind the shed."

David nodded. "Who were these people who last saw her . . .? Evelyn, and . . ."

He shrugged. "I don't know their names. Carlina's got a lot of interested boys. She's very pretty. Everyone loved her. So good. All the boys wanted to know her. I never could keep track of them all. She was dating this guy for a few months, but she never seemed too serious about him. He seemed nice enough, wanted to help find her . . . " He trailed off for a moment. "Brandon, I think."

David wrote that down. "Your daughter went to Oak Cliff High?"

"That's right."

"Did she know Marlene Dotts?"

He nodded slowly. "Not well. I think they were friendly, though. They were in a couple of the same classes I think, knew a lot of the same people. They played soccer together."

That was it. More than enough to tie these cases together. If, indeed, the murders were committed by the same person, it meant the killer had become active again. It was likely someone tied to the school. And that meant this case was theirs.

Briggs would be *pissed*. But too bad.

He pulled a business card from his wallet and handed it to Mr. Adams. "Thank you. I'll be in touch if there's anything else. But please, if there's anything else you think of, the FBI will be handling the investigation from now on."

"You will?" he asked in surprise. "All right, great. Thank you, Agent."

David looked around the house, at all the family pictures—mom, dad, and Carlina. She was a smiling, beautiful girl, with sparkling green eyes and light hair. Yes, it made sense that she'd had a lot of admirers. Again, he felt a tug at his heartstrings.

"Hey," he said to the father. "Mind if I peek in her bedroom?"

He shook his head. "Upstairs. First one on the right."

He climbed up the stairs and into a teenager's normal, messy bedroom, strewn with clothes and clutter. Looking around, he began making a mental note of the things he'd want the police to confiscate. She's probably had a cell phone on her. The first order of business was to get that unlocked.

As he stood there, his phone buzzed with a text from another agent, Dick Charles, an older guy who was right on the cusp of retirement and spent most of his day behind his desk, counting down the days. *Hey. You were looking into something with Kevin Reynolds, right? The detective from DFW?*

He quickly thumbed in, *Yeah, what about him?*

Murdered.

Hunter studied the message. Shit, this would not be good news for Mia. *What happened? They catch the guy?*

Got his brain bashed in by his own baseball bat. A witness saw a woman in a green sweatshirt leaving the scene. That's all they got to go on.

He shook his head, thinking about her. Just another setback that would keep her from learning the truth and getting back on the beat with him.

Too bad. Right then, he could've used her.

Mia loved to go after the cold cases. Especially the ones that involved the murder of young girls. It was due to some personal tragedy she'd had as a child. She never mentioned it, but he'd learned more about it during her trial. Supposedly, her sister had been kidnapped and murdered, which was why she'd gotten into the FBI in the first place.

And Mia had a different way of looking at things—she was intuitive, seeing things that most investigators overlooked.

A case like this would be right up Mia's alley.

It could more than get him in trouble—he could wind up in jail, too, for aiding and abetting a wanted criminal. But if it could save another life and put this killer behind bars? If it could give Carlina's parents some peace? It would be worth it. He'd tell Mia it would free him to help her out—something he couldn't do with his boss breathing down his neck.

Yes, a call to his partner was definitely in order.

CHAPTER FOUR

Mia North sat on the edge of the bed in a sleazy hotel room off of Interstate 20 in Terrell, east of Dallas, watching her lunch spin on a microwave turntable.

She'd been there one night already, which meant it was time to get a move-on. She couldn't spend more than forty-eight hours in any one place. While she still had to stay nearby so she could look for clues to clear her name, she couldn't risk the police finding out where she was.

Tonight, she'd have to leave.

But not before I eat, she thought as the microwave in the kitchenette dinged. She opened the door and pulled out a cup of ramen noodles.

Fine dining.

Honestly, she couldn't remember the last time she'd had a nice, leisurely meal. Despite all the crap she'd been shoveling in her mouth—Twinkies at a rest stop, KFC drive-in food, a hot dog from a roadside food truck—somehow, she was losing weight. Her clothes hung loose on her, and her face looked positively skeletal.

She twirled the noodles around the tip of a plastic spork and opened up a map, trying to decide where to go, next. She'd thought about getting a tent and going camping somewhere near the Cedar Creek Reservoir. People at campsites usually left their neighbors alone. She could stay there, be close to Dallas, and plan her next move.

Then, she did what she always did, when she was thinking about where to go next.

She grabbed her phone and typed in *Wilson Andrews.*

The scumbag who'd landed her in prison to begin with. She had a fantasy of catching up to him, of giving him his due. And now, with Kevin gone, it seemed only right that she focus on him. If only she could get close to him.

No new articles. Last she'd heard, he and his wife had taken a trip to Aruba, laying low after the capture of his crazy brother, Jerry Andrews.

He was probably still there. And was it even possible to get near him, with his security detail, and his many *friends* in high places?

Sighing, she tossed her phone down and pulled the map closer to her. She circled her next stop on the map, then leaned back against the headboard, sighing. An old episode of *The Facts of Life* played on the television set—Tootie had done something bad.

As many times as she'd told Kelsey not to watch crap television, not to eat junk food . . .now, that was all she was doing.

But she had bigger things on her mind.

How was she going to get in touch with David to see if there were any updates on the Ellis Horvath case? He had a burner phone that he'd gotten, just for them to keep in touch, but he hadn't been answering his calls.

As she sat on the drab flowered comforter, slurping noodles into her mouth, her burner began to ring on the night table.

She glanced at it.

Of course, it was a strange number. All numbers were strange, since this wasn't her phone.

She picked up. "Hello?"

"North. It's me."

Her heart skipped. "David?"

"Yeah. That's right. Calling you from a payphone."

"Wow. You found one? Good for you!" She smiled, glad to have a friendly voice to talk to. "Wait, what about your burner?"

"Lost it. I'm going to get another one you can call me on. I'll get you the number—"

"Fine. I'm happy you called. I need to talk to you. That lead you gave me . . . Reynolds . . ."

"Yeah. I heard. He was murdered."

"Yep. Do you have any information on it?"

"No. Sorry, I've been a little preoccupied with other things, but I'll look into it more, if it'll help you," he said. "The only thing I heard was that they saw a woman in a green sweatshirt, I think, leaving the place."

She groaned and looked down at her green sweatshirt. She had an errant dehydrated pea on her chest from the noodles. "That was me."

"Yeah?"

She sighed. "I went to his place to see if I could find any evidence. And I found him. His head had been smashed in. He'd been dead a couple days, I think."

"Jesus. You think that one of Andrews's friends did him in?"

"I don't know. Probably. Andrews doesn't want anyone squawking about what he did to frame me. Maybe he thought Reynolds was under too much pressure to talk. But you know they're never going to pin anything on him. I'm sure his brother's getting the royal treatment in prison, right now."

"Yeah. I'll bet. Scumbag. I hear he has the best lawyers money can buy."

"No doubt. Luckily the case against him is pretty iron-clad. There's no way he'll get off. At least, I hope." She shuddered at the thought. She, once, had thought there was no possible way she'd be convicted for murder, and yet, here she was. "So, I need something else. Something more to go on, David. Help me."

"I'll try, but . . . I have something else going on."

She blinked. So he hadn't just called to check on her and make sure she was okay? "Why? What's up?"

"It's another case, and Pembroke's pretty hot on me to act on it. There was a girl who was murdered. Do you remember the Marlene Dotts case?"

"Dotts," she murmured, mostly to herself. It came to mind right away. Most cases that involved a young, murdered girl did. "Oak Cliff, right? She was strangled."

"That's the one."

"Still unsolved, from what I remember. They went to the high school and asked around. No one seemed to know anything. All her friends' alibis checked out. There were no witnesses. They decided it had to be a random transient passing through the area. By the time we got our hands on it, all the leads had gone cold."

He whistled. "Wow. You have a way better memory than I do."

She sighed. Sometimes she wished she didn't. She wished the details of these cases didn't hang so heavy in her mind. Maybe then she could sleep better. "So what about it?"

"Well, there's been another murder, almost identical."

"Another?"

"Yeah. Same neighborhood. Same MO. Same everything. The girls even knew each other at Oak Cliff High. Now, I have no idea why the killer would wait a year—and it is a year, I checked, the anniversary's next Tuesday—but it's really looking like these two murders are somehow connected."

Mia blinked. Now that was a mystery. Two similar murders, of two high school girls who knew each other, in Oak Cliff? Yeah, that probably wasn't a coincidence. "What's the girl's name?"

"Carlina Adams. She was strangled, too, and found behind her parents' house this morning. Her dad said that she'd gone to a friend's house around the corner to watch movies with a couple other guys, and she must've been snatched on the way home."

Mia clutched the phone, anxiety spiraling through her. Samuel, her brother, had been nine, when he'd been snatched. It was just a moment of carelessness. Her mother had been in the department store, looking for drapes. Sam Jr. had been in the toy aisle, looking for a Transformer to add to his collection. She'd left him there, for a minute, maybe two.

And in those few instants, life had changed forever the Clopecki family. Mia, her older sister Francie, her mom and dad . . . their lives had been ripped apart.

"You're intrigued, I can tell," David's voice came over the line, stirring her from her thoughts.

"Yes. Of course. Duh, you know me! If I was still an FBI agent, I'd be all over it."

There was a pause. It was in those few moments of silence that it hit her.

"What?" she snorted. "Don't tell me . . . "

"Well . . . I know you're probably bored to death, huh?"

"Um. You really think I can help you, David? I'm kind of otherwise occupied."

"If anyone can help, you can."

"Come on. I'm not exactly in the ideal place to help anyone. I can barely help myself. I can't go around solving murders in my free time."

"Why not? That guy in that movie did it. Harrison Ford. He tracked down the one-armed man, all while fleeing Tommy Lee Jones, then found out it was his old buddy, the doctor."

She rolled her eyes to the cottage-cheese ceiling. "This isn't a movie. I don't see a happy ending here."

"Mia . . ." he said, his voice low. "I really need your help. Briggs— he's the guy in charge of the police— is really giving me sh—"

"Oh, God. Not him! Sorry."

"Yeah. I know. He's brutal with the FBI."

"Not just the FBI. Francie used to work under him, until she requested transfer. And Briggs was a big reason my dad put in to retire.

There was a case he was working on that Briggs got wind of—the two locked horns pretty bad. Otherwise, I think he'd still be working there."

"Yeah. Then you know. He's being a total pissant. I'm trying to compile evidence, and Briggs is setting up a wall, making things difficult for me. Pembroke doesn't like me . . ."

"Pembroke doesn't like anyone."

"He liked you. Me, he tolerates. But if I make one wrong step . . . I'm screwed. I have like, zero hope of solving this case without your help. Besides, if you help me with this case, I'll be able to help you with yours."

She sighed. He always seemed to be so down on himself. Ever since his divorce, he'd lacked confidence. But she hadn't done anything he couldn't do himself. Now, he could do a lot more than she could, on the run from the authorities. He was a free man, at least. "I can't do anything, David, and you know it."

"I know you can. You don't have to worry about rules. Right?"

"Just because I'm a fugitive doesn't mean I'm going to go all Wild-West-shootout on the world. I'm still a law-abiding citizen . . . for the most part."

"Okay. But that poor girl . . . she was in college."

Mia swallowed hard. Not only did it make her think of Kelsey, but she'd experienced loss like that, firsthand. Carlina's parents were probably beside themselves. Just as her own parents had been, after Sam. It was a miracle that they somehow stayed together. This kind of thing usually destroyed marriages as much as it destroyed lives. So many lives, the lives of everyone the murdered person knew. "What can I possibly do from here?"

"I can let you have the files. You can look them over. I know you. You might be able to see something that we missed. That's all. That's all I'm asking. Nothing more."

She inhaled. That wouldn't be too terrible. Still, she had enough on her mind. "I don't know . . ."

"Mia. What if this killer is just getting started? What if he's looking to kill again?"

That was true. She never could sit well, knowing there was a murderer out there, looking to strike again. Not when she knew the details of the case and had the ability to stop it.

It pretty much sealed the deal. She leaned over and stirred her noodles with a fork, then threw it down, her gut roiling with a new kind of hunger. It was the same feeling she'd had when Sam was killed. A hunger for justice.

"Look," he said. "I've got to go. I'm late for my kid's baseball game. Are you in, or not?"

She felt a twinge of pain in her heart. Kelsey was in basketball, and she'd missed every one of her games this season due to this nightmare. If she could help David with this case, maybe she'd clear enough off his plate so he'd have time to help her with her own case.

"All right," she said. "I'll just take a tiny look. Where do you want me to pick up the files?"

CHAPTER FIVE

After checking out of the motel, Mia pulled up at the Scrub N' Shine 24-Hour Car Wash in downtown Kaufman at a little after nine. Sure enough, the place was empty.

That was the problem, these days. Everything was under video surveillance. Even outdoor spaces, like neighborhood parks. Anything they did, they had to do it with the expectation that they were being watched. It had made these last few weeks absolutely hair-raising.

She sat in the lot across from the car wash, waiting for David to arrive with his dark sedan and reading an article that had just appeared in the *Dallas Observer.*

DALLAS - The DFWPD says an 18-year-old Oak Cliff girl was found murdered on Tuesday afternoon.

Police responded to a 911 call at about 6:00 a.m. of a body found on the 20000 block of Maple Street in Oak Cliff.

They found Carlina Adams dead in the backyard of the home she shared with her parents. She had been strangled.

Adams was a first-year student at Tulane University and had graduated from Oak Cliff High School last year, with honors. "Our family has lost a bright star," OCHS Principal James Higgins said. "A member of the soccer team and NHS, she was known by many for her vivacious personality and spirit. She will truly be missed."

During a press conference, Lieutenant Gunther Briggs of the DFWPD said that every possible avenue would be investigated in order to bring the murderer to justice. Copeland Adams, Adams's father, pled for information leading to the apprehension of the murderer.

"My daughter is a very special girl. She lit up every room she went into. Please, if anyone has any information that will help us find her killer, I beg you to come forward," he said. "Her mother and I will never be the same."

This safe Oak Cliff neighborhood is especially on edge, considering this is the second murder of a female teenager in a year. Last March, Marlene Dotts, 18, was found murdered only two blocks away from the location where Adams was discovered. Dotts's murder remains unsolved.

Asked if the two cases had any correlation, Briggs replied, "While we're investigating every possible connection, we have no reason to believe so, as of now."

There have been no arrests and no other details were immediately available.

Mia read the words, shaking her head. Briggs was such an idiot. Two crimes like that? Of course they were connected. He was just posturing because he didn't want to admit he didn't know what the connection was. Three words the guy would never say: *I don't know.*

She scrolled down to a picture of the girl—fresh-faced, pretty, with a curtain of bangs that fell in her sparkling green eyes. Her smile was contagious, real. She had a bit of mischief in her eyes, too, like she knew a secret that she refused to tell.

Yes, Carlina Adams was probably a very popular girl.

But that only meant people noticed you . . . it didn't mean everyone *liked* you.

And someone clearly hadn't liked Carlina. Mia refused to believe this was some transient. No . . . there was a secret here. A big one. And two girls were dead because of it.

When Mia looked up again, she saw Hunter's sedan, heading to the drive through lane. He fed his dollars into the machine, pressed a button, and then got out of his car, carrying a dark shopping bag. His car continued to roll on, into the car wash, and he went inside the building next door.

Her turn.

She pulled up into the space behind him, fed her dollars into the machine, lined the car up on the track, shifted to neutral, and stepped out, pulling her hood up over her head and tying it tightly around her face.

She quickly went inside the waiting area. It was empty. She looked around and noticed just one security camera, facing the other way. David was there, hands in his pockets, staring into the window that provided a view of the cars in the washing lane. She noticed he hadn't shaved in a while—the beard didn't really fit him.

He turned to her for barely a second, made a quick motion to the coffee service there, and winked.

Then he opened the door on the other side of the building and disappeared.

She followed his motion to the coffee service. Sure enough, he'd left the bag there.

She turned, poured herself a cup of coffee, then nonchalantly swept down, grabbed the bag, and headed for the door. As she did, she took a sip of the coffee. It scalded her lips.

When she got to the end of the track, her piece of crap car—she'd have to trade it in soon—was still a piece of crap, but it was cleaner than it probably had been in ages. She quickly got in, put the coffee in the cup holder, the bag of files on the passenger seat, and pulled toward the exit.

David was already gone, like a phantom.

Her one friend in the world. Her one connection to the life she'd had. She wished she could've said more to him, but that wink was all they could afford.

Dammit, she thought, hitting the steering wheel with the heel of her hand. She hated this. This cloak and dagger bullshit.

Desperation and sadness over her lost old life threatened to invade, but she shoved it away from her mind. When she stopped at a red light, she opened the bag and peered inside. Lots of files—David had been thorough.

And a small, fluorescent-green Post-It note on top.

She peeled it off, turned on the light above her, and read: *Call when you can give me your thoughts. And DON'T EVEN THINK OF GOING NEAR THE CRIME SCENE! It's crawling with people you can't afford to run into. – D*

That was probably very true.

Still . . . the best way to solve a crime? Visit the crime scene. That was FBI Basic Training.

And so tempting. She couldn't deny it. The photographs only told part of the story. To really understand it from all sides, the scene of the crime was the best source of evidence.

But in order to solve a cold case, when much of the evidence was either gone or reduced to second-hand reports, she had to make do.

And so she would.

For now.

But if she needed to . . . she really couldn't put it past herself to get close to the scene of the crime, just to get the full picture.

Which meant that she should probably turn back now. Tell David sorry, but he'd have to work this one on his own.

But then she glanced over at the photograph of the dead girl and sighed. She was already invested. There was no stopping now.

*

The Hillcrest Motel was yet another dive, this one right outside of the Dallas city limits. This one was really bad, with shag carpeting and orange and brown-flowered bedspreads and matching drapes, almost like it hadn't been updated… ever. But her wallet had been running thin for the past few days—she was down to her last hundred, and the Hillcrest had a value rate of $29 a day. She'd gotten something off the Chik-fil-A value menu—another great meal that would do a number on her stomach—and settled down cross-legged on the twin bed to review the files.

As she nibbled on a waffle fry, she paged through the file on Carlina Adams. Because the murder was relatively new, there wasn't much information yet. But David had done a good job of compiling it.

Carlina Adams was the daughter of Copeland and Lucy Adams. Her father was an auditor at one of the nicer hotels in downtown Dallas. According to an interview with him, he'd been at work that night when he received the call that she was supposed to return to her friend's house, but had disappeared sometime during the night. A number of them had gone out, early in the morning, looking for her, only to find her shortly before sun-up, dead behind her parents' shed.

There was an interview with Evelyn Rhinehart, as well. She said that she and her boyfriend, Fred Watkins, and Carlina and her boyfriend, Brendan Crenshaw, had been in the middle of watching movies when Carlina suddenly remembered she'd left the windows open in her car and decided to run back, alone, to check them. She was supposed to return, and never did. At first, Evelyn had thought she decided to stay with her mother, but she wasn't answering her texts. Only at two in the morning did she finally contact Carlina's mother, who said she hadn't seen her all night. They'd begun a search, which only lasted a few hours before the girl was found.

Nothing very groundbreaking. The interview with Brendan and Fred, too, were just more of the same. All of them corroborated Evelyn's story, almost perfectly. The three of them had been together until two, when they decided to go out looking for the girl. At that point, they'd conducted a search, not finding her until sun-up.

There were pictures of the crime scene, the girl, curled into fetal position, bruises on her throat. Mia went through all of them carefully, trying to see something that others might have missed.

Still would be better to have been there, she thought glumly, closing up the file and grabbing a chicken nugget.

She pulled the thicker file toward her. This was the one on Marlene Dotts.

She remembered the case well.

Marlene had simply been heading home from soccer practice at school, at dusk. She lived only a mile from Oak Cliff High School, and her father and mother had gotten their lines crossed, each one thinking the other was going to pick up Marlene. In the end, no one did. Her friends had offered her rides, but Marlene was very conscious about her appearance, according to friends, and told them she'd walk to get more exercise in.

Video surveillance from a coffee shop about halfway through her route showed her passing by. She was walking with someone, but the person's body was behind Marlene's, so no identification could be made. But Marlene's pace and posture were both relaxed, so it was decided the killer was likely someone she knew.

Suspicion had almost immediately fallen upon Rick Loos, her soccer coach, who was the last known person to see her alive.

Mia read through the interviews, recalling the work she'd done. During the investigation, it was learned Rick had been a bit squirrelly. Mia recalled that he'd made some inappropriate advances and remarks to the girls on the team.

Mia scanned the margin, where David had written: *Rick Loos—Deceased.*

She grabbed her phone and looked it up. Sure enough, Rick Loos, who had been discharged from both his teaching and coaching position after news of his inappropriate conduct had come out, had died in a drunk driving accident, only a week ago. Apparently, he'd been leaving a Dallas bar, intoxicated, and wrapped himself around a tree. Instant karma.

But it meant that he hadn't murdered anyone, and the killer was still out there.

And did his death have anything to do with the recent murder? Had the killer felt the need to go dormant when heat was on the coach, but once the coach was dead, was inspired to resume his work? If so, why?

It was definitely a mystery. So many thoughts and ideas crowded her mind. She needed to talk them over with someone to straighten them out.

She lifted her phone and was about to call David, but set it down.

He'd tell her "thanks for the help, I'll take it from here." He'd tell her to stay away. He'd try to talk her out of investigating and finding out more information on her own.

And she'd be smart to heed his warnings.

But she couldn't do that. Oak Cliff was practically just down the street.

And it felt like it was calling to her.

CHAPTER SIX

Early in the morning, in his hotel room outside of Dallas, U.S. Marshal Kane Wilcox studied the file on Mia North for the hundredth time, trying to see what made this woman tick.

He knew about her family—all of them, in law enforcement. He knew about Samuel, Jr., who'd been abducted from a department store when he was nine. He knew that she'd been top of her class in college and at Quantico. He knew that she had made a name for herself, solving cold cases, and was a respected member of the team until she'd gone off the rails over this stalker case.

That had to have been a shock to the people she worked with. Ten years with the Feds, ten years of busting cases and following the rules, only to murder a lowlife scumbag in cold blood?

Supposedly, the guy, Ellis Horvath, had been stalking her kid, a cute, freckled little girl named Kelsey.

Can't say he blamed her very much.

But still, rules were rules, and they'd joined the Feds to uphold them. He'd wanted to end plenty of lowlifes in his time.

You had to know when to walk away.

He scrubbed a hand through his graying, bristly hair. He'd last been in the military almost thirty years ago, and he still couldn't picture himself wearing his hair any other way than the high-and-tight, and pulled out his cigarettes, ready to step outside and have his morning drag, when he noticed something.

It was a photograph of a footprint in the mud of the safe house, outside the lake where Jerry Andrews had met his end.

Small. Delicate. *Female*. Not a child's, either.

This last case, where Jerry Andrews had been apprehended for a couple of kidnappings? It had her name all over it. The guy, brother of a senate wannabe, might've been completely off-his-rocker, but he'd managed to avoid detection a long time. He'd killed a couple of FBI agents, too.

The story that they'd put forth, that this David Hunter guy—Mia North's former partner—had saved the day?

No. He was sure Mia North had been there.

She'd heard her family was in trouble, and she couldn't leave it alone.

Not to mention that she was a fighter for justice. Just like he was. There was a good bet that if she saw a case—especially with a young victim involved—she'd look twice. Sam Jr. probably demanded that of her.

He twirled the cigarette in his fingers and turned the pages, reading more about David Hunter. They'd been partners for a long time. Kane hadn't had a partner for a long time, but he knew that if you were lucky enough to have a good one that you could stick with, the bond was unbreakable.

And he could bet anything this David Hunter had covered for her, that night at the safe house.

Plus, she had a daughter. A husband. People she'd do anything to protect. No matter what the cost.

He smiled at the photograph of the slight woman with dark hair and light eyes—graduation day at Quantico. She looked like a mother, and yet, she also looked like a cop. Tough. Like she could handle herself in a fight. She might not have had the brawn, like some agents, but she looked scrappy. There was a determination in her eyes that was hard to resist.

You have a big heart, Mia North. And I bet you're here, somewhere. That big heart of yours won't let you go too far away.

But where would she go, first? Friends, or family?

He decided on the latter.

Making a note of the address, he shoved his cigarette back into the sleeve, pocketed it, grabbed his jacket, and headed out to his car.

CHAPTER SEVEN

Oak Cliff hadn't changed much since the last time Mia North had been there.

The neighborhood that Carlina Adams lived in was full of modest, middle-class homes from the early 20th century. They were spread out, most on hills, under the shade of plenty of mature oak trees. It was a nice place to raise a family, relatively crime free.

Of course, Mia knew that even the safest places had sordid histories. She'd briefly looked into Marlene's case, a year ago, but she'd also investigated a missing child case here at the beginning of her career, going on almost nine years ago. Georgia Franklin, from what she remembered, was a smart, outgoing nine-year-old who'd disappeared from her bedroom one night. When all the leads dried up and no new clues were found, the police's official explanation was that the girl had run away.

Mia, however, fresh back from maternity leave after having her own daughter, refused to believe that. It was one of the first cases she'd worked with David Hunter on. They were two of the only people who believed the parents when they said they feared something terrible had happened.

And they'd been right. She'd worked round the clock, trying to find leads, and had finally broken the case, after a month. It was one of the first cases that had established Mia as an agent who could work magic with cold cases.

Back then, when things were normal. People had respected her as an agent, looked up to her. She felt a stab of pain in her heart at the thought. She didn't know how good she'd had it.

But having worked this town before meant that the streets were familiar to her. The old Pizza Hut was there, as well as the Adult Books store. The Texaco gas station, the Wal Mart. It was all just the same. She drove past Oak Cliff High School, a sprawling, modern structure, also situated on a hill. By now, both students and teachers had probably been rocked by the news of the latest murder. She imagined the two girls, kicking across the soccer field, and she thought of Rick Loos.

Was there something to him? Was his death really accidental? It seemed like a lot of tragedy to befall a school in such a short time.

She let GPS guide her to the Maple Lawn development, where both Carlina and her friend Evvie had lived their entire lives. It was more of the same—a sprawling house with yellow shingles and black shutters—old but well cared-for. She slowed to a crawl outside Carlina's house. The neighborhood was dead. There were no police cars there, only yellow tape, stretched near the backyard. The nearest neighboring homes on the road were barely within view.

Still, it felt like too much of a risk to park outside and go poking around the yard, considering a murder had just taken place there.

Hmm, she thought, craning her neck to see around the house. The home backed up to mature woods. *I wonder if I can somehow get around that.*

She looped around the block and realized that there were quite a few worn paths through the grass, into the woods. Pulling to the curb, she looked around to make sure no one was watching. Then she stepped out of the car and hurried into the forest.

The paths were heavily trodden, and muddy. Footprints were everywhere—they'd be no help in finding the killer. When she was deep inside the woods, she had to look around to orient herself. From there, she could barely make out the shingles of the homes. One of these houses was Evvie's, she knew, but she wasn't sure which.

She spied the house with the yellow shingles and tried to find the path that would take her there. Predictably, the muddy footprints seemed to multiply as she got closer. That made sense, since people had been out on the path, searching for Carlina.

There was a fence in the backyard, as well as an old swing set. Yellow tape surrounded it. She moved closer, all the while checking to make sure no one was watching her.

The place behind the shed, where the body had been found, was looped with yellow tape. She moved and peered over the fence, until she could see. It was nothing but mud and decaying leaves. She studied her surroundings, scanning everything carefully for the slightest overlooked clue.

If there had been any evidence left behind by the killer, it was gone now.

From there, she looked around, trying to recreate the crime in her mind. The unsuspecting girl, walking home late at night. Why would she do that, in the dark, with the rain? Why hadn't that boyfriend of hers taken her? Had they had a fight? Maybe there was something to that. She wished she could interview that kid. David probably already had, and had come up with nothing.

Because, as suspicious as it was, it could also be nothing at all. The reason could simply be that she was just a teenager. They didn't always think things through, make the best decisions.

She imagined Carlina coming down the path, heading for her house, for whatever reason. She imagined the killer, lying in wait. Probably behind the shed, or crouched behind a tree or the fence. She imagined the killer springing on her from behind, wrapping the ligature around her throat, pulling tight. She imagined the fear, the question of who could be killing her, wanting her dead. Did she know her assailant? The photographs of the injuries suggested she'd been murdered from behind.

So, not the same as Marlene. Or was it?

Marlene might've been walking with someone she knew in that coffee shop surveillance footage. But that didn't mean that person had killed her.

Maybe both had been killed by someone they didn't know.

But why would that someone have waited? What, if anything, did the coach's death have to do with it?

Maybe Rick Loos knew who the killer was. Maybe he had to be silenced. Or maybe he had killed Marlene, but someone else killed Carlina? She felt like the answers were there.

Turning, she made her way out of the forest, making plans to look into Rick Loos some more.

*

Mia decided to take her research to an empty park tucked at the end of a side-street. It was actually a nice day just before Spring had fully sprung, so there was plenty of sunshine, and after dealing with all this heavy stuff, she needed something to cheer her up.

Usually, that was Kelsey. Kelsey always brightened her day, like a salve that took away all of those jaded thoughts she had about the deterioration of society. How could the world be all bad when something as beautiful as that little girl existed?

Now, though, every time she thought about Kelsey, her heart twisted.

As she sat on the park picnic table, she looked out at the mama and baby ducks, traversing the pond, and thought about the last time she and Kelsey had gone to the park to feed the ducks. Kelsey had loved the babies so much, she'd wanted to take one home with her.

"That would be terrible, don't you think? Taking them away from their mommy?" Mia had asked.

Kelsey had thought about it, long and hard, a little crease appearing above her bright blue eyes. "Yes, mommy, you're right. They should stay right where they are. A family. I wouldn't want to be away from you, either."

She blinked the memory away and found she had tears in her eyes, which scattered down her cheeks. Kelsey had to withstand so much in the past few months. It was too much for anyone, much less a nine-year-old.

Wiping them away, she opened up her phone and perched it on the picnic table, then typed in *Rick Loos.*

An article came up right away: *Current and former soccerl players detail inappropriate behavior by OCHS coach, lack of action by administration*

She clicked on it. As she read along, more of the story came back to her.

Some of the girls on the team said that he was inappropriate at times. One player said he would "constantly ask people if they were late to their Special Olympics practice." And though Loos was married, he'd texted Marlene relentlessly, messages that ranged from longingly romantic to sexually explicit to abruptly aggressive.

Included in the report were screenshots sent in his prolonged attempt to develop a relationship with Marlene. In one message, he'd texted her, "I keep having this dream of you showing up on my doorstep after my wife goes to work. I want to make love to you in the mornings… just wondering if you would be into it. Good way to start our days off." Several messages later, he confessed, "Babe, you're all I think about. I can't hide the fact that I adore you any longer."

Marlene had denied or ignored the advances that came through text. Her responses included remarks like, "Gross," "So inappropriate," "Yeah okay you should know better than to do that," and, in part,

"You're my coach and you should have never let yourself feel the way you do. I did nothing wrong."

A couple players on the team said that the advances went beyond just texts. At one point, one of them saw him grab Marlene's buttocks as she exited the team bus. Some of the girls said that he was singling her out, grooming her for a relationship.

Marlene, however, had never complained about the treatment, which was probably because she was hoping to get into Stanford, and she didn't want to upset her chances. When Rick Loos was questioned, he repeatedly denied doing anything wrong. He also vehemently denied murdering Marlene.

But the texts were all there, courtesy of Marlene's cell phone. He was the last person to see her alive, too. He had admitted to asking her if she wanted a ride home, but said she'd declined.

Still, he'd been the prime suspect, especially when someone mentioned that they saw him and Marlene getting into an argument on the sidelines, during practice. She'd been screaming at him, *I'm going to tell* and *You can't treat people that way! It's just not right!*

Yes, the guy was a total jerk. Mia would've loved to see him put away, for a long time, on the basis of being a complete creeper alone.

Surveillance video outside the high school showed Loos's car there until much later at night, way after the time of death, and a couple athletes had reported seeing him in the locker room at around the time of the murder. Since his only contact with Marlene had been lurid texts, he hadn't even been charged with unlawful sexual contact with a minor, much less murder. He was relieved of his job, though, and though he'd stayed around Dallas, he had pretty much dropped out of public life altogether.

So from the start, Mia had really doubted that he was the murderer. And if he didn't murder Marlene, then there was a good chance that both murders could have been committed by the same person.

She would have to look into Carlina's life a little more. Classes, activities, friends. Maybe she could find another connection.

But that meant doing something dangerous.

She dug through the papers that David had given her, looking for something in particular that she'd seen earlier. It was a fragment someone had written in there, but she'd found it interesting. *Copeland and Lucy Adams are going to stay with her mother in Fort Worth for now.*

So the house on Maple Street was empty.

She sucked in a breath and let it out as she watched the ducks fly away. *Yes, I'll do it. If it's the only way, then it's the only way.*

CHAPTER EIGHT

Mia's car idled in front of Carlina's house.

Sure enough, it looked unchanged from earlier in the morning. No one was there. No cars in the driveway. Shades drawn tight.

She gnawed on her lip, trying to decide what to do. She'd been straight as an arrow, before she became a fugitive. She wasn't too fond of the idea of adding another breaking and entering charge to her rap sheet.

But even though she was, like she'd told David, a law-abiding citizen, for the most part. . . they still thought she was a criminal. So she could do this.

Finally, she decided to make her move.

She pulled down the street and hurried to the house. She went around to the back door and took out the hair pin she'd brough with her, especially for this reason. After a few tries, she heard the mechanism inside click, and with a quick look around to make sure no one was near, pushed on the door.

It opened and she slipped in, carefully looking around. The place was full of homey, farmhouse décor, and smelled a little like a cinnamon stick. Scattered among all the pine boughs, checkerboard print, old milk cans, were many, *many* photos of Carlina. The girl seemed to watch her as she moved through the living room. She stopped in front of an old player piano that was covered in photographs of the girl, the most notable one a poster-sized print of her at her high school graduation. Pretty, yes, with strawberry-blonde hair and pink lips, in that photo, she looked a bit like a young Heather Locklear. There was another picture next to it, with a few ponytailed girls on a field, holding soccer balls under their arms and smiling for the camera.

Mia looked around a bit more. Whoever Lucy Adams was, she kept a clean house. Everything was spotless. And she'd been a good mom to Carlina. The refrigerator contained a snapshot of their lives together—magnets from different places they'd been to on vacation, photos of happy family holidays, a college report card from Tulane—straight A's.

Mia crept down the hallway, listening. The only sound was the ticking of a clock, somewhere. She climbed the carpeted stairs to the second floor. At the top of the stairs, she found a room in purple zebra-print.

She hovered in the doorway, her heart near giving out.

The bed was unmade, zebra comforter balled at its foot, and letters above the bed spelled out CARLINA. Things here were much more cluttered, with trash and piles of clothes and shoes on the ground.

It was as if Carlina had merely stepped out, and would be back at any moment.

Her mother probably desperately wanted to clean the place, but wanted to give her daughter space, too. And now that she was gone—well, Mia decided Lucy Adams couldn't bear to come in here at all. No wonder they'd left.

The room smelled like an overly sweet, rose perfume. Over the dresser, there were piles and piles of make-up. There was a mirror covered with stickers, with movie tickets and photographs tucked under the frame. Most of the photographs were of her and a girl with blonde hair that was long on top and short—almost shaven, on the sides.

Mia crossed a thick, purple shag rug and looked around at her desk. David had probably confiscated things like her cell phone, but for some reason, they'd left her laptop there. *David, hello? What were you thinking?*

He was probably thinking that anything they needed to know, they could get off the cell phone, and that the laptop would only have college papers and assignments on it. Cell phones were such treasure troves. But girls loved to delete information from the cell phones. Laptops, they sometimes forgot . . .

She didn't have to think about it long. Their loss was her gain.

She picked it up and shoved it into her bag.

As she turned to leave, she thought she heard a sound downstairs. She'd been almost relaxing, but now, when she heard the noise, Mia jumped to high alert. Quickly, she took the steps down, but it was a false alarm. There was no one there.

Not wasting any time, she escaped outside and rushed for the door. She couldn't wait to see what evidence she could find on Carlina's laptop.

CHAPTER NINE

The Hi-Glo Diner, outside of Dallas, was all retro chrome and tile. Mia was glad that it was mostly empty when she arrived. "Just sit anywhere, Honey," the old waitress said, waving at her from behind a counter.

Mia passed a revolving dessert case, the check-out counter, and a long bar with red vinyl-covered stools, and slid into a corner booth in the very back of the establishment. It was the safest place; there, she'd be able to open up the laptop without anyone looking over her shoulder, and see everyone as they came in.

The waitress, wearing a tight-fitting blue dress that seemed ready to pop open, her hair done up in a messy bun, came lumbering toward her, carrying a glass of murky-looking water and a napkin-wrapped package of utensils, which she set down on the table. She had a nametag that said Flo, because *of course* her name was Flo. She looked like the average diner waitress from any old television sit-com, right down to the gravelly voice and the pencil tucked behind her ear.

Mia should know—she'd been watching far too much TV Land in those motels, and always seemed to stumble upon *Alice*.

"Hi, Honey," the waitress said, not looking up from her pad. "What can I get you? We're have everything except the Salisbury steak special."

In her excitement, Mia had forgotten to look at the menu. "I'll just have a cheeseburger," she said, and her stomach grumbled in protest. *Like I need another one of those.*

"Fries and vanilla shake?"

"Sure." *Might as well do the trifecta of heart disease.*

"You got it," she said, spinning on her heel and heading for the kitchen.

As Mia reached for the laptop, a song came on the jukebox in the corner. It was Johnny Cash's "Folsom Prison Blues."

She winced as she thought of those months she'd spent in prison. It'd been a long time. The only thing that kept her going was Aiden and

Kelsey, and knowing that, after the trial, she'd be set free. Because *of course* she would be. She was innocent. Justice would prevail.

Unfortunately, that wasn't what happened. Through a series of misfortunate events, she'd been found guilty, and handed a life sentence.

But she'd had to escape. She needed to find out what happened, and clear her name. No one else was going to be able to do it. No one else was even trying to find Ellis Horvath's real killer. And he was out there. She was sure of it. Free, while she was on the lam.

Here, though, nearly two weeks later, she was still running around like a dog, chasing its tail.

She paged through the selection of songs on the jukebox attachment at her booth, picked out, "Girls Just Want to Have Fun" by Cyndi Lauper, fed a dime in, and hoped that one would play soon. Kelsey had always loved that song.

Then she opened up the laptop and pressed the power button, hoping it wasn't password-protected.

It wasn't. It hadn't even been turned off. When it turned on, the first thing she saw was Spongebob wallpaper. She touched the keypad and noticed several open tabs.

Clicking on one, she found her messaging app.

It only had a few messages in there. One was to a professor at Tulane—*Do we have to use primary sources for the paper, or are secondary sources ok too?* The professor had responded: *Primary sources preferred, secondary as necessary.*

There were a couple more messages, but they all appeared to have to do with school.

That was it. Dull.

She navigated out of that tab, to the next one, for her Instagram. Her profile picture was a photo taken at her high school graduation. She was wearing a cap and gown and standing with a tall, handsome boy, proudly displaying their diplomas. Her name was CarlinAA26 and her About Me section said, *b <3, Tulane '26, gsoc 4ever!*

Whatever that means, Mia thought glumly, but then realized it wasn't that hard. B was Brendan, her boyfriend. Tulane was her school. Girls' soccer.

Okay, so who was B? Hadn't David mentioned someone named Brandon?

She clicked around and saw more pictures of her with the tall boy. One of the pictures was taken at a beach. She was wearing a bikini and sitting next to a hotel pool with him, and the caption was, *Brendan and I aren't coming back! Spring Break Life is THE life!*

Brendan, her boyfriend, was a pretty good-looking kid. They made a nice couple. It looked like they'd been dating a while. So, pretty serious.

Someone named *BrenCren123* had commented, *UR HOT!!* And she had replied with another heart emoji.

Mia clicked on BrenCren123's profile. Sure enough, it belonged to Brendan, the kid who, for some reason or another, hadn't walked his girlfriend back to her house.

He profile said: *c<3, OCHS FOOTBALL ROCKS! Livin' the dream here in Dallas.* There was a picture of him standing in front of a fancy red sportscar.

Here in Dallas. No mention of college. So he wouldn't be too far away, either, if she wanted to go ahead and somehow find him . . .

She wondered if she could do that.

She stared at a picture of the two of them, hugging, wondering what else there was. It seemed like her life was too perfect. Too rosy. People always did put their best foot forward on social media. There had to be something she was hiding. Especially if she had a mother that seemed intent on coming in her room and "tidying up."

Of course.

Carlina was no idiot. If she thought her mother was hovering over her shoulder, she'd delete anything incriminating. Anything she didn't want people to see.

Mia navigated to the trash bin and smiled. There were 437 deleted items in there.

She hovered over the button that said *Recover deleted items?*

Yes, please.

When she clicked on it, an assortment of files appeared, from deleted text messages to emails.

She clicked on the first one, an instant message conversation with someone named only D: *Hey, when are you showing your pretty face around Dallas again?*

Carlina had replied with a flirtatious: *What, are you telling me you miss me, baby?*

D: Yeah. It's been a long time.

Carlina: Well, I'm thinking of coming back in March. You want to get together?

D: You have time?

Carlina: I have to hang with E and B, and visit with the parents. But I could make time for you.

D: You're still dating that prick?

Carlina: It's complicated.

D: Like I'm not.

Carlina: ☺

D: Still has to be our secret.

Carlina: Why? It's not wrong.

D: I told you. I don't want to get into it.

Carlina: My lips are sealed.

D: K. Call when you get in.

Mia stared at it, balling her hands into fists in front of her. So she was seeing someone else. A mysterious D. This was interesting.

She opened up message after message, but there were no more from D. She did find one interesting message exchange between Carlina and Brendan, that had taken place in June of the previous year.

Brendan: You're so cold, Car. You know that?

Carlina: What do you mean?

Brendan: I waited for you outside the lockers for an hour but I found out you'd just left without me.

Carlina: Oh, boo hoo.

Brendan: F said he saw you with someone else. Are you cheating on me?

Carlina: Give me a break. Really? You believe F over me? He's such a douche.

Brendan: I would never cheat

Carlina: Right. You forgetting February? You hooked up with me behind M's back the whole month. Remember?

Brendan: It takes two.

Carlina: Oh yes, I made you do it. You're such an innocent. Whatever, dude. She'd probably still be alive if you'd been with her. Face it, you've NEVER been able to keep it in your pants, bro.

Another bombshell. Mia stared at the words, comprehension leaking. Brendan had dated both Marlene and Carlina around the time of Marlene's death?

Brendan was a little bit of a player. And jealousy was always a great motive for crimes of passion. Was that what this was?

If so, that was huge. And Carlina clearly didn't like Brendan as much as those photos, and the little <3 B on her social media, seemed to suggest.

Now I really, REALLY wish I could talk to this kid, she thought to herself, shaking her head. If she was still with the FBI, she'd have been knocking down the kid's door already.

David was probably already on it. He wasn't as experienced as she was, but he had a good head on his shoulders. They complemented each other.

Still, *she* wanted to be the one to interrogate these people, asking the right questions to get them to reveal themselves. David would even admit that he wasn't as good at it as she was. And sometimes, solving a crime could come down to something as simple as asking the right questions, at the right time.

She looked up, her jaw still hanging open, and realized her hamburger, fries, and shake were sitting next to her. When had they gotten there? She grabbed a fry. Cold. So . . . a while ago. She reached for a straw and was about to plunge it into the shake when her eyes drifted to the door.

Two Dallas police officers were walking in.

Her stomach dropped.

She watched as Flo said, "Hey, Bob, hey Jeff, sit anywhere you like!" The two scanned the place. Mia sunk down behind the screen of the laptop, trying not to make eye contact. Her heart thudded against her ribcage. Of course, they turned her way and started to walk toward her.

Oh, God, she thought, trying to act natural. She took a sip of her shake and played with a French fry, but by now, she felt like anything she ate would be coming right back up. *I've got to get out of here.*

She pretended to check the songs on the jukebox machine at her table as the two men strode toward her.

Without warning, they hung a quick right and headed toward the bar and slipped onto the vinyl stools.

She quickly packed up the laptop and scrambled in her wallet for a twenty. Slapping it down on the counter, she rose to her feet, just as Flo was coming back to check if she needed anything.

"You sure weren't hungry, were you? Guess that means you don't want none of our famous cherry pie," Flo said with too loud a voice, scooping up the twenty. "I'll be back with your—"

"Keep the change," Mia said softly, scooping up her things and heading for the door.

She'd almost made it to the counter when a male voice behind her called, "Miss?"

She stiffened. For a beat, she wondered if she should make a run for it. No, that would be even more suspicious. Pressing her sweaty hands against her thighs, she turned, trying to keep as nonchalant as possible, even though she could feel her heart getting ready to give way. "Yes?"

The two officers were staring at her.

She wasn't wearing a hood. Had forgotten the dark sunglasses in her car. She'd dyed her hair, but other than that, she wasn't wearing much of a disguise at all. They were going to recognize her. This was it. The end. She'd be carted off to prison within the hour.

But the older of the two officers simply pointed at her table. "You forgot your phone."

"Oh!" She turned back. Sure enough, it was right there, where she'd left it. She rushed back and pocketed it. "Thank you, officers."

She hurried outside as fast as she could, cheeks heating, and never looked back, barely even breathed, until she'd driven far away. Once she calmed down, she made the decision to give David Hunter a call.

CHAPTER TEN

In the tech department of the Dallas-Fort Worth FBI Field Office, David Hunter paced back and forth, thinking.

Not just about the case, unfortunately.

He'd missed most of Louie's game, gotten there when they were in the bottom of the ninth. Just in time to see his son miss a pop fly.

Needless to say, Louie wasn't happy. He was on his son's shit-list, big-time. He'd have to find some way to make it up to him.

But at least he'd gotten the files over to Mia. Hopefully, she was having a better time sorting through things than he was.

Now, though, they were about to have a breakthrough. He felt sure of it.

The guy at the lab table, an IT genius named Mark Hollins, huddled over the device, fingers working madly. He gave David an annoyed glance over the rim of his glasses. "Would you quit it, dude? You're making me nervous."

"Sorry," he said, pausing for a moment and leaning against the table.

He always got impatient when things were out of his hands. He alone could do nothing to unlock Carlina's cell phone, but he knew it would bring answers. Answers he couldn't wait for.

Speaking of answers, he checked his phone again, wondering if Mia'd had a chance to go over the files. Knowing her, she'd cracked them open the second she got them in her grabby little hands. So why hadn't she called him, yet? Was she in danger? Maybe it was just a simple case of her not finding anything new.

Meaning the dead girl's cell phone was of prime importance.

"Dude. Quit it."

David stopped moving. Without realizing it, he'd begun to pace the floor behind Mark's stool again. "You got anything?"

"One second . . . and . . . there. *Voila.*"

Mark handed him the phone, now open to him like a treasure chest.

So he did exactly what one would've done with a chest of treasure. He dove in eagerly, hungry for anything it could give him.

First, he opened up her messaging. The last person she'd texted, predictably, was her boyfriend, Brendan Crenshaw, on the evening she died:

Brendan: U back yet?

Carlina: Yep

Brendan: When can I see you?

Carlina: Not sure. Really busy . . .

Brendan: Seriously?

Carlina: Fine. I just heard from Evvie. She wants us to go to her house for movies tonight at 8.

Brendan: K. I'm in. I'll pick you up.

Carlina: It's fine. I'll walk.

David cringed. That sounded like a real match made in heaven. About as cold as day-old mashed potatoes. Weren't teens fond of using heart emoticons and crap like that? There was none to be found in any of her conversations with the kid. Was there trouble in that paradise? He had to wonder.

"Everything you hoped and dreamed of?" Mark asked, spinning on his stool.

"Well . . . no. If it was, it'd say, *My killer is so-and-so,* and make it easy on me," he said with a smirk, scrolling down.

The next one down the list was Evelyn Rhinehart, her best friend. She'd also been texting with her on the evening she died. The second he opened it up, there were the emoticons he'd been looking for. Lots of smilies and dead faces and ones he'd never seen before.

Evvie: You there yet?

Carlina: Just got in!

Evvie: Come over and watch horror movies with Fred and me tonight. I'll get pizza.

Carlina: Sounds good

Evvie: Want to bring Brendan?

Carlina: Ugh, do I have to?

Evvie: Haha. 8 pm?

Carlina: Sounds good

The next message was to her mother, Lucy Adams. She'd sent it from the road, something about how the traffic on I-20 out of Shreveport was at a standstill, and how she'd be a little late. There was a long list of other messages between mother and daughter, showing that either Carlina was a very caring daughter who didn't want her mother to worry about her, or that her mother was controlling and didn't want Carlina going anywhere without her permission.

David was just trying to decide which when his phone rang from an unknown number.

He glanced at the area code.

It was Mia.

He held up a finger to Mark, scooped up the phone, and took it out of the tech lab, checking to make sure the hall was empty before answering. "Yeah?" he said in a low voice.

"Hey."

"Hi. You got the files. What'd you find?"

"The boyfriend, Brendan? He dated both Carlina and Marlene."

"What?" That was a bombshell. He'd gone over those files backward and forward and couldn't remember seeing anything that even resembled that. "Is that a guess or . . ."

"It's a fact."

"How do you know?"

There was a pause. "You don't want to know."

Oh, hell. That meant she'd done exactly what he'd told her not to. Had she gone to the crime scene? "What are you, girl? Begging for trouble?"

"I couldn't help it. In any case, it paid off. I think you should interview Brendan again about the connection. I would, if I could."

"Yeah . . . actually, I was about to do it, anyway, but for another reason. I just got her phone open and from the tone of the messages, it seems like there was trouble between them."

"I don't doubt it. I think she had another guy on the side."

"Yeah? Who?"

She chuckled. "I can't do all your work for you." Then she added, "Seriously, I don't know. I just saw some IMs that were between her and a mysterious person named D. They happened two weeks ago."

IMs. Hell. He'd seen the laptop in Carlina's room, but had opted to take just the phone, instead, since teens limited most of their communication these days to phones. So did that mean she'd actually . . . *Hell.* Talk about taking chances. "And how did you find that out?"

He braced himself for the answer, but she simply said, "You don't want to—"

"Know. I get it. And you're right. I don't. You need to be careful. Stay away. You're helping no one but the bad guys if you get caught. You gotta get back to that little girl of yours."

She sighed. "Yeah. I know." A longer pause. He guaranteed she was thinking about her family. "You've been checking up on them, right?"

"Often as I can. Yes, Ma'am."

"Thanks. And you'll check Brendan Crenshaw out?"

"Yep. On it."

"I'll call you later to find out how it goes."

"Got it. Just you promise me one thing?"

"Sure."

"Step back a little, okay, girl? You know what happens when you get too close to the fire."

She let out a long, uneasy breath. "I'll try."

She wouldn't. He knew her. Balls to the wall, all the time. That was the way she always worked. When he thought of her, he usually thought of her from the back, her ponytail swishing on her head, because she was always two steps ahead of him.

And if she got apprehended, now, it would be all his fault. He was the one who'd convinced her to take on this case, knowing how invested she would likely get.

He ended the call then and plugged Brendan Crenshaw into his phone. He needed to find the kid's address and pay him a little visit. He just hoped his partner wouldn't try to do the same thing.

*

Brendan Crenshaw lived in a house that most people would've believed was pretty swanky.

David stared at the sprawling stucco mansion from the front seat of his car, where he was stopped at a gate, waiting for security to deign to look at him.

The guard finished what he was doing on his computer screen and turned to David. "Can I help you?"

David flashed his credentials. "I'm David Hunter with the FBI. I'd like to speak to Brendan Crenshaw, if I may."

The man's eyebrows lifted. He held up a finger and slid a partition closed, then picked up a phone. A moment later, the partition opened. "What's this in regard to?"

He frowned. *What do they think it's in regard to? How many other crimes has this kid been close to?* "The murder of Carlina Adams." When the man stared blankly at him, he added, "His *girlfriend*?"

"Right." The partition closed once again, then opened once again. The massive iron gates in front of him also slowly began to part. "When you get up toward the house, stay to the right. Someone will meet you out front."

"Thanks."

Sure enough, when he passed the long barrier of thick bushes and came to a C-shaped driveway with a fountain in the middle of it, a white-haired man in a suit was standing there, waving at him to go to the right. He did so, parking next to a limousine and a black McLaren. He got out, eyeing the car with appreciation. "Whoa, that's really a fine—"

"Mr. Hunter?" the man said, striding toward him. "I'm Harold Hopper, the Crenshaw's butler. I'll take you in."

He followed the man into a massive foyer with a sweeping staircase and checkerboard floors. The butler took him through high arched doorways to a sitting room with an entire wall of windows, overlooking a lake with its own dock. David Hunter gaped. *I think I got into the wrong business.* "What is it that Mr. Crenshaw does?"

"I own Crenshaw Frozen Foods," a voice said from somewhere in the vast room. So far away was he, Hunter only noticed the man when he stood up and began walking toward him. "You've probably eaten some?"

"Tater tots, right?" David asked. He never bought that shit, even though Louie always begged for it.

"That's right," he said, offering his hand to shake. "I'm Edward Crenshaw, and this is my wife, Olivia."

He motioned to a woman who was so thin, it looked as though a stiff wind would blow her over. She was pale, sickly, and looked less-than-thrilled to see him there. She nodded his way, a cold distance in her eyes.

"Nice to meet you . . .," he said, looking around. "I believe I said I wanted to talk to Brendan, though. Not you."

Edward Crenshaw's smile was thin. He thrust his hands into his pockets and rocked from heel to toe. "Well, that's just it. He's not here."

"Where is he?"

"At the gym, probably. Our boy's an athlete. One of the best in the state."

Hunter nodded. "All right. Which gym?"

"Hold on, there, Mr. Hunter." His smile widened. "Look, I think you have the wrong guy, if you think our Brendan had anything to do with this. He didn't."

"I understand. And I do understand your desire to protect him. But this is really just standard procedure."

Mrs. Crenshaw's eyes widened. "But he didn't do anything wrong!" she cried.

"No, no," Hunter said, holding out his hands to appease her. "I didn't say he did anything wrong. I just need to get his side of the story so that we can piece together what happened to Carlina."

"You don't seem to understand, though," Mr. Crenshaw said. "Brendan's . . . a bit high-strung. He gets very nervous. And he's under a lot of pressure right now."

"He's in college?"

"No . . ."

"He didn't decide to go on to college after high school?"

Crenshaw's jaw stiffened. Mrs. Crenshaw said, "Bren decided to take a gap year. We encouraged it. Last year was very stressful for him."

"Because of Marlene?" Hunter asked.

The two exchanged glances. "Yes," his father said, reluctantly. "Because of Marlene."

David opened his mouth to ask more about their relationship but Mr. Crenshaw took his arm and guided him to the door.

"I'm sorry, but like I said, we really can't help you, since Brendan's not here, and—"

They stopped short when a young man appeared in the doorway, breathing hard, looking like he'd seen a ghost. "Dad," he said. "What are you doing?"

The man gritted his teeth. "I told you to stay upstairs. I told you we'd take care of this."

Brendan shook his head. "Are you the FBI agent?"

David nodded. "Brendan Crenshaw?"

"Yeah," he said, looking at his parents. "Mom, Dad . . . I'll handle this."

His father looked angry, but said nothing.

"Come on," he said, motioning to a door. He led David outside, to a garden. When they were far enough away from the house, he turned and said, "Sorry about my parents. They're trying to keep me sheltered. But I told them I want to talk to you guys. I want to clear my name."

"Good, I appreciate that. They said you took it very hard, after Marlene's death."

He nodded and ran his hands through his scrubby blond hair. "Yeah. We were dating two years."

"And Carlina?"

"Carlina and I started dating after Marlene died. It was kind of a shared-grief thing."

"And how was your relationship with Carlina?" David asked.

He shrugged. "I don't know. Fine, I guess. Ups and downs."

Right. This kid isn't being straight with me. "You should know that we've gotten hold of Carlina's phone and checked her messages. And it reveals some things that make it look like maybe it wasn't so fine?"

His eyes widened, and he looked away, his hands shaking. "Well . . ."

David leaned forward and lowered his voice, taking the tone he'd use to address Louie after he make a mistake. "Son. I know you're nervous. But it's better if you just come clean now. You'd not going to be able to hide anything from us. If we don't know it already, we'll figure it out eventually."

He sighed, "Fine." He shook his head. "I had a feeling Marlene was cheating on me. So I got together with Carlina. I was with Carlina when Marlene was killed, so I blame myself. That's why . . ."

"That's why you decided to take that gap year?"

He nodded miserably. "Carlina didn't understand. She kept calling me a loser for not being able to move on. She moved on so easily. But she didn't know Marlene like I did. They were rivals, in a lot of ways." He sniffed and wiped an unshed tear from his eye. "And now, with Carlina. . . I wonder if someone's trying to frame me for this. But I swear, I didn't touch either of them. Like I said, I was with Carlina when Marlene was killed, so I couldn't have--"

"Unfortunately, she can't vouch for you," David said in a low voice.

He stopped. Swallowed. "Yeah. I guess not. But I was with Evvie and Fred when Carlina—"

"I have a note here, some conflicting testimony that I've gotten. I think this comes from Fred. He originally said you were with them the whole night. But then he said that you went out looking for her, when she didn't return, at around one? And you returned at around three? Her body wasn't found until six. By then she'd been dead a few hours. The coroner estimated her death at between one and four AM."

Horror dawned on his face. "So what are you saying? That I could've . . . I didn't. I just went looking. Because I—I loved her."

Maybe he did. The look on his face was earnest. But the kid struck David as someone who tried too hard. A nice kid, but one who'd work and work to make a girl like him, no matter how much she put him down. "These texts on her phone. And her calling you a loser? Excuse me for saying so, but she didn't really appear to return that sentiment."

The look on his face was utter devastation. "Yeah," he said in a small voice. "I don't know. I kept trying to recreate what I had with Marlene. But they were different people. Marlene was really sweet. Carlina could be cold. Mean. I mean, she was a nice girl but then, she had that side to her that would just . . . go off. She was really calculating. Manipulative, sometimes. I got the feeling she was . . . you know. That there was someone else with Carlina, too."

He raised an eyebrow. "Some would say that would be your motive for killing them. Jealousy."

"But I didn't," he insisted. "I swear it."

David nodded; he wasn't one of the people who'd say such a thing. He believed him. Brendan seemed affable. Not-too-bright. But the jealous type? No.

"All right. Then who did you think this other lover was?"

He shrugged. "No clue. In either case."

"Did you know their soccer coach, Rick Loos?" David asked.

He nodded. "Yeah. It wasn't him. Marlene always told me he was a creeper. Carlina said that, too. All the girls thought he was one, because of the way he treated Marlene. Singling her out, and stuff. They used to call him *Dick* Loos, because they all knew his reputation for playing around with the girls."

David remembered what Mia had told him. *I just saw some IMs that were between Carlina and a mysterious person named D.* Two weeks ago. Could that have been Dick Loos? "Did you know if Carlina was in touch with him at all, after he was let go from his coaching position?"

"I can't believe she would be. When Marlene died, we all really thought he was to blame. Half the team had seen them arguing, right before she walked home."

"Do you know what about?"

"Carlina said that she said something about how *he shouldn't do that. That it was making it hard to play the game.* She said she was going to tell. We all thought she meant his old tricks, grabbing and touching the girls and making inappropriate comments toward them. Nothing new. What was new was that Marlene was taking him to task for it. She was quiet. But she was the one he singled out, most of all. I think because he knew he could get away with it, with her."

"I see. So in your mind, there was no doubt he was guilty?"

"Yeah. I thought he'd be arrested the second it happened. Only the police couldn't find the evidence they needed to put him away. Carlina said that once the police got after him and he lost his job, he texted a couple of the girls, trying to talk to them, but that he kind of faded off because the police were suspicious of him. But he didn't text Carlina, because she pretty much told him that she thought he was a disgusting pig. Carlina liked to speak her mind. And now . . . I don't know. Besides, he died a week before Carlina was killed. So it can't be him." He shrugged. "I really don't get it."

"Who do you think killed Carlina, then?"

He let out a burst of bitter laughter. "I don't know! I mean, the truth is, most guys had a thing for her. Fred was with Evvie, but even he said he'd wanted to get with her. She was just that kind of girl. Kind of irresistible. But infuriating. I figure any guy who'd kill her would do it because he couldn't have her, because she insulted him so much." He frowned. "Marlene was quieter. Sweeter. She didn't have a mean bone in her body. So to me, that's the real question. Marlene didn't make enemies."

David nodded and stood up from the bench, then looked out at the peaceful lake. A couple of ducks were sitting upon it, but other than that, it was a mirror-flat expanse of gray.

When he looked down at Brendan, the young man seemed like he was struggling to say something. Finally, he said, “When I couldn’t find Carlina, I was pretty pissed. I felt like she left me, maybe to go see that other guy she was seeing, so I wandered around. By myself, trying to figure out whether it was over for us. So no, I don’t have an alibi, but I swear I didn’t do it.”

David nodded again. The kid was scared to death, and maybe he was hiding something, but it didn’t feel like murder. He’d also had an alibi for Marlene’s murder. If he was an actor, he was a very good one.

Brendan Crenshaw wasn’t the killer.

He’d have to go back to the drawing board.

He said goodbye to Brendan and went back to his car, thinking. His best bet was to see if he could find more about this mysterious character, D. Was it Rick Loos? Or someone else entirely?

CHAPTER ELEVEN

Mia sat in the front seat of her car, eating a Playa Bowl—her stomach couldn't handle any more French fries and she thought the acai would do her good-- and reading the news of the day from the *Dallas Observer.*

The front-page headline read: *More Questions than Answers in Hunt for Oak Cliff Killer.*

Oak Cliff – Police and FBI have yet to name a suspect in the murder of an Oak Cliff teenager, whose body was found yesterday in her backyard. Carlina Adams, 18, was found strangled to death in the backyard of her home on Maple Street.

They have also not yet said if they believe this murder is connected to a murder of Adams's classmate, Marlene Dotts, last year.

"At this point, we have a lot of questions, and few answers," Dallas Fort Worth Police Lieutenant Briggs said.

She snorted. There was nothing there she didn't already know. She was used to knowing far more than what the papers said. This was infuriating.

She scanned down to another article on the bottom of the front page, and groaned. *Senate Hopeful Wilson Andrews Poll Numbers Remain Strong.*

Well, wasn't that great for him.

The bastard was lower than low. He'd tried to pin a number of crimes on her in order to help out his psychotic brother, Jerry, who was now—only because she'd investigated as a fugitive—going to serve a long prison sentence. But Wilson Andrews had come out scot-free. Clean. And he still had a good chance of getting elected.

She groaned again at the thought. If only she could find a way to prove that he was responsible for Ellis Horvath's death!

She knew it was true. She just couldn't find that smoking gun.

If she could, she'd go free. But with Reynolds dead . . . it seemed impossible. She had no leads whatsoever. The case was dead in the water. Her only hope was to have David Hunter dig something up from the inside, and for that to happen, she'd have to get this case solved and off his plate.

Frustrated, she crumpled up the newspaper and went back to staring at her burner phone, wondering when and how David Hunter was going to get in touch with her. At least this was one case where she could make a difference.

But she needed her damn partner's help to do so.

She licked blueberry juice off her fingers and picked up her phone. She put in a call to him.

It went right to voicemail.

Damn. He'd said he was going to interview Brendan Crenshaw four hours ago. He should've been done with it by now.

And of course, here she was, in the dark. How could he expect her to help if he didn't feed her the information?

Well, she wasn't *totally* in the dark. She had the laptop. She had IMs from this mysterious D, and Evvie.

Evvie.

Evelyn Rhinehart.

Now that was a thought. If anyone would know Carlina's deepest, darkest secrets, it would be her best friend.

Out of curiosity, Mia went through the files she had and, sure enough, came across Evvie Rhinehart's address—1531 Cypress Street.

It was all too easy. Almost as if it was begging for her to pay them a visit.

She looked down at herself. If she took off the hoodie and dark sunglasses, she would almost look exactly like her old, professional self. Minus the badge, though. But she could fudge that one. Besides, very few people actually asked to see her credentials. Once they heard FBI, their minds always went to, *Am I in trouble?* Not, *Can you prove who you say you are?*

She tilted the rearview mirror down and wiped a little blue smudge from the corner of her face. Despite all these weeks on the run, she still looked human. Maybe she was only a shadow of her former self, but it could work. She could still pass as FBI.

David would be pissed. Obviously. But then again, maybe he should've kept her apprised of his investigations. Maybe this would teach him—if he wanted her help, he needed to play by her rules.

Making the decision, she started up her car and headed toward Oak Cliff.

When she got to the development, she pulled to the side of the road in front of the house, a modest ranch. It looked empty, with no cars parked outside. She stepped out, tucking her blouse into her jeans, and walked to the door.

She knocked. A moment later, a girl with big blue eyes and cropped blonde hair opened the door. She had long, dangling earrings and was wearing a retro THE CURE t-shirt.

"Evelyn Rhinehart?"

"Yeah?" Her ambivalent expression gave way to a frown. "Are you the police? Because my parents aren't home."

"I'm FBI actually," she said, pausing for a moment. This was where she'd say her name, but she hadn't thought of one beforehand. Thinking quickly, she added, "My name's Veronica. Veronica Lake."

Her nose wrinkled, just as Mia cringed with the realization that Veronica Lake was an old-time movie star. But Evvie simply moved aside and said, "I guess you can come in."

She led her to a living room with a massive sectional and big-screen television that took up most of the real estate there. Then she curled up in a corner of it. "I guess you want to ask me questions about Carlina?"

She nodded. "That's right. I heard that you two were best friends?"

"Yeah. We were. I was probably one of the last people to see her alive. She was right here, with me, Brendan, her boyfriend, and my boyfriend Fred." She looked around and shuddered. "We all love horror movies. We were having a movie marathon."

"Can you tell me what happened?"

"Yeah. She came here a little after eight, and we started watching the movie. But like, halfway through it, it started to rain. So she said she thought she left the windows open in her car and wanted to go home and make sure they were closed." She shrugged, "Her parents were always getting on her for not being responsible, and the car was new, so . . . I gave her an umbrella and she left."

"And she didn't come back. When did you realize something was wrong?"

"Like, thirty minutes afterwards. We were all talking, because she was supposed to come back so we could watch Friday the Thirteenth. At first, I thought she'd stayed to talk to her mom, since her mom was upset that she'd just gotten home and wanted to run out with friends, instead of spending time with her. So we decided to watch the movie. But then she still wasn't back, so I texted her mom."

"And her mom said she hadn't seen her, right?"

"That's right. So by then it was around one. And yeah, originally I told police that the three of us—Brendan, Fred, and I— were together the whole time, but then I remembered that Brendan went out to look for her and couldn't find her. He was gone like two hours. When he came back, we all went looking. We only found her when the sun came up." She shuddered again. "Well, her father found her. Behind the shed, I guess. I didn't want to look. It's so horrible."

"Did you know Marlene Dotts?"

She nodded. "Not well. They were all on the same soccer team. I don't play soccer. But I guess she and Carlina were . . . not friends. Rivals, I guess? Frenemies? I mean, sometimes they were friends. Carlina said some pretty mean things about Marlene. I don't know what that was about. But at the end, like the month before she died, they were a lot closer. When she died, Carlina took it really bad. Said she was one of her best friends. That kind of thing."

"Did Carlina ever mention her coach, Rick Loos?"

She nodded. "Said he was a creeper. But not really to her."

"Do you know of someone with the initial D that Carlina might have been seeing?"

Evvie frowned. "D? No . . ."

"Was she seeing someone other than Brendan?"

Evvie sighed. "Yeah. I got the feeling she was. But she never told me who it was. She was really secretive about it. I thought it was because she was also seeing Brendan, and she didn't want word to get back to him."

"And did she have any enemies?"

Evvie winced. "Honestly? She had a lot."

"She did?"

"Yeah. Not really enemies, but people didn't always like her."

"That's interesting," she said, looking up. "What makes you say that?"

"She was outspoken. Manipulative, in a way? Like, she could spin a story, convince people the sky was green. And sometimes it rubbed people the wrong way."

Mia nodded. This fell in line with some of what she had heard about Carlina in the past. "Did it rub Brendan the wrong way?"

She shrugged. "When I first heard she was dead, I thought it might have been Brendan. He went looking for her, earlier, and he was gone so long. I texted him, and he didn't respond. And he was really pissed off when he left here. He and Carlina were kind of on the outs. Fighting all the time. And he can be a little possessive. I'd thought he was the same, with Marlene. He was constantly keeping tabs on her. But Carlina told me it couldn't have been Brendan. They were together when she was killed."

"They were? She wasn't just saying that to protect him?"

Evvie snorted. "You don't know Carlina. She wouldn't say anything to protect him. If he was guilty, she'd gladly throw him to the wolves. Their relationship wasn't all roses and sunshine. He felt guilty for not being there for Marlene, and Carlina was the one who doled out his punishment. She treated him really bad."

"Why were they together, then?"

"Brendan's popular. Rich. The quarterback of the football team. He's the guy any girl would want as her boyfriend. So Carlina used that."

"She dated him for the reputation?"

Evvie nodded. "Yeah. Pretty much. It wasn't really a secret that she treated him badly. I think everyone knew. And he's one of those guys . . . the worse he's treated, the more he tries to make up for it, win her favor. So I guess he looked a little pathetic in the end. But he's a sweet guy. He's definitely not a killer."

"What about her other enemies?"

"Blair."

"Blair?"

"Yep. Blair Evans. She was on the soccer team with them. When Coach Loos was constantly favoring Marlene, Blair was jealous. She was the one always trying to stir up stuff, saying how Marlene was pursuing him, using him to be first string on the team, since she was only a mediocre player to begin with. She said the same about Carlina, too, but Carlina put her in her place. I truthfully think Loos was scared of Carlina, because if he tried anything with her? It'd be front-page news and he'd lose his job in a second."

"Did you know about the argument Marlene had with Coach Loos?"

"Yep. Carlina told me all about it. It was actually about something Blair had said. Blair was constantly taunting Marlene, telling her that the reason she got special treatment was because she kept spreading her legs for Coach Loos." Evvie shrugged and pulled the blanket tighter around herself. "And Marlene got sick of it. She didn't want him to keep singling her out. So she finally called him out on it."

"Interesting. You think she might have had something to do with their deaths?"

Evvie shrugged. "If you asked me if anyone I know could commit murder, I'd say no. But of everyone, I think Blair is closest. Wait." She stood up, went to a bookshelf, and pulled out a yearbook. She flipped to a picture of the soccer team from last year and pointed to a picture. "That's Blair, and there's Marlene and Carlina. Tell me what you think."

Mia studded the picture closely. Sure enough, the girl with the dark, curly hair was staring daggers at the backs of the heads of the two girls in front of her. If looks could kill . . .

Unfortunately, they couldn't. And a simple stare wasn't enough to go on.

"But Rick Loos was fired from his job after Marlene's death, right? So Blair had no reason to kill Carlina, did she, if she was jealous about him favoring the other girls?"

"Well . . . it was more than that. Blair just hated Marlene and Carlina. And she's home from school, too. I think she went to some college in New Jersey, but the news is she flunked out, first semester." Evvie chuckled, "Now she works at the McDonald's on Oak Lane. She's a jealous, vindictive bitch, that girl."

Mia made a note of the name. It was a lead. Was it possible that this Blair Evans held Carlina and Rick Loos responsible for her failing out of school, and wanted to exact some revenge?

Weirder things had happened.

Evvie shrugged, "Anyway . . . why are you asking me all this? Didn't you go through her diary?"

"Diary?"

She nodded. "Carlina was always writing in her journals. She kept them in her bedroom. Under a floorboard, she said. She probably wrote all about everything in there."

"Really?"

"Yeah. But her mom was a snoop, so she said she might burn them. She said her mother would kill her if she knew what was in them. So maybe she did burn them."

Mia sighed. If only she'd known about them when she'd been in the house, before. She made a note of it and stood up. "Well, thank you for your time," she said, turning to the door.

She stopped when she noticed a woman in a short bob and raincoat, standing in the doorway, staring daggers at her. "Evvie. What is this? Who is this woman?"

"Mom," Evvie said, standing up and throwing off her blanket. "This is . . . I forget her name. But she's from the FBI."

Mia nodded. "Hello, Mrs. Rhinehart, I'm—"

The woman was holding a shopping bag in each hand. She set them down and said, "Can I see your badge?"

Mia's blood ran cold. "Well . . ." she skirted around the woman and headed for the door. "I seem to have forgotten it, in the car. I was just leav—"

"What's your name again?"

"Um—I'm just going to be on my way," she said, quickening her pace toward the door.

"You're a reporter, aren't you?" Mrs. Rhinehart snapped, following her. "You all have the nerve, don't you? A poor girl is dead! And you don't care. You just want your scoop, don't you?"

Mia turned around briefly when she reached the door and pulled it open. "I'm sorry," she said, stepping through the door.

"Yeah, you should be! I'm calling the police."

"No, that's not necessary. I'm sorry I—"

She pulled out her phone and made a show of dialing it.

Mia turned and, as fast as she could, ran across the lawn to her car. She slid into the front seat, started the ignition, and tore out of the development, her hands shaking on the steering wheel.

About a mile down the road, she turned into the parking lot of a paint store, clutching the wheel until her breathing returned to normal. Then she checked her cell phone.

Of course. No calls from David. He wanted her help, but he didn't want her getting herself caught. So he'd likely not involve her at all, again. If she was going to be of assistance to him, she'd have to do it on her own.

Blair Evans. It was another lead, yes. But could she pursue it without putting herself in danger? If she was smart, she would simply hand it off to David and wipe her hands of the whole business.

She couldn't do that, though. Not with the murder still unsolved, and a hot lead, waiting to be explored.

She'd just have to be more careful in the future.

CHAPTER TWELVE

Mia drove up to the Oak Lane McDonald's, trying to determine how to best check out Blair Evans without endangering herself.

She idled there until a car pulled up behind her and beeped. Finally, she went ahead, into the drive-thru lane and spoke into the speaker. "Just a coffee."

"A dollar thirty-nine," a female voice said. "Pull to the first window."

When she got to the first window, she looked for a girl with curly hair. But it was an acne-faced kid with a nose-ring. She sighed and handed him a five.

He handed her the change and she moved ahead, sighing. The coffee at these places was terrible. And Blair probably wasn't even working today.

But when she pulled to the second window and the partition opened, she was surprised to see a girl with a dark, curly ponytail.

"Hullo?" the girl said with attitude, thrusting the coffee out farther out the window. "Are you going to take this, or what?"

"Oh. Yes," she said, taking it and setting it in her cup holder. "Thank you."

"No problem," the girl said. Mia wanted to ask something else, but the girl gave her a look, and snapped her fingers. "Um, move ahead, please."

Mia lurched ahead, and then drove around and parked in a spot, trying to figure out how to proceed. Should she go in, order something, and wait? As she was about to do so, the door closest to the parking lot opened and Blair walked out, pulling the tie from her curly mane and shaking it out. She yanked off her apron, threw it all in the passenger-side of her old Chevy Impala, and got in, then sped away.

Mia pulled out and drove, hot on her tail.

She was used to pursuit, so she knew to stay a few car-lengths away from her target. She followed the girl for about a mile on the main drag of a busy road with a lot of stores and traffic lights. A couple of times, she had to zoom through a light just as it was turning red, but eventually, the Impala turned in to a shopping mall. The girl pulled into the parking lot of a Macy's and parked.

Mia found a parking spot a few rows away, stepped out of her car, and quickly followed her into the lingerie area of the store.

There, she peeked out from behind a display of bras and saw Blair, trying to decide between a red and a pink silk teddy. Then, she went and grabbed a black lace nightie.

I wonder who those are for? Mia thought as she hid behind a rack of robes.

A moment later, Blair turned toward her. Mia shrunk back.

Then she was on the move, headed toward a fitting room.

Mia quickly followed close behind, stepping into the large fitting room as an old lady was walking out. The woman looked at her strangely, and she realized it was because she didn't have anything to try on. She quickly grabbed the first thing she could find—a giant FUN FACT: I DON'T CARE t-shirt.

As she was about to head in again, she nearly ran headfirst into a body, coming out.

She saw the dark, curly hair, and stiffened. She backed away to find Blair Evans staring at her with a scowl, hand on one cocked hip. "Why are you following me, creeper?"

Shocked, Mia backed away and caught sight of her reflection in a floor-to-ceiling mirror. Dark glasses, hoodie pulled tight around her face, intense expression . . . Blair was right. She definitely looked like a creeper.

She cleared her throat. "Blair Evans?"

"Yeah . . . who are you?"

Her cover blown, she set aside the t-shirt. "I'm a . . . private investigator. Investigating the murder of Carlina Adams."

Blair's over-plucked eyebrows went up. Behind her, an old lady with a squeaky-wheeled shopping cart gasped and pushed the cart into high-gear to get away from them, it's squeak-squeak-squeaking quickly fading away.

"I don't know anything about a murder," she said, backing away like a scared, cornered animal.

"You didn't know Carlina Adams?"

Her eyes volleyed around the store, as if she was looking for someone to save her. "No . . . I did. We went to high school together. But I haven't seen her since graduation."

"And Marlene Dotts?"

The girl pressed her lips together, and they trembled. For a moment, Mia thought she might cry. But then she said, "I saw her on the day she died."

"I've spoken to someone who said Marlene had an argument with your coach, Rick Loos, and that your name came up during it? That's very interesting."

"Who said that?" Her eyes went wide. "I don't know why it would."

"Come on, you do know. Is it true that you and the two victims didn't get along?"

She scowled. "You seem to know everything, already. Why are you even bothering to ask me questions?" she said, fluffing her dark hair. She sighed and put her lacy lingerie on a rack. "Look. Yes, we didn't get along. Marlene was constantly flirting with and hogging our coach's time. So he was spending all of his time with her, ignoring the rest of us. And it was seriously affecting our performance. She wasn't all that good, and he kept putting her on first string. She was a teacher's pet. So we all thought that she was probably sleeping with him."

"And that's what the argument was about?"

She shrugged. "Probably. She probably didn't like that the rest of the team resented her for being the coach's favorite. And since I was the one who was most vocal about it, I guess that's why my name came up."

"And Carlina? You didn't like her, either?"

"Ugh. She was worse. She was a bitch. The two of them were popular, pretty . . . typical nightmares. Most of the girls on the team couldn't stand either of them. I can tell you they probably all celebrated when they found out . . ." She stopped and seemed to realize who she was talking to. "Anyway. I didn't like either of them. But no. I didn't kill either of them, if that's what Evvie's insinuating."

Mia looked up in surprise.

"It was Evvie, wasn't it? Saying those trash things about me? She never liked me, either," Blair said with a sigh. "I'm sure she's probably laughing her ass off at me that I'm home, now, working fast food instead of studying at NJIT. I bet she told you I couldn't cut it. But the truth is, I came home for another reason."

"And what's that?"

"Love."

Mia waited for her to say more, but when she didn't, she asked the inevitable question. "You're in love with someone? Who?"

She smiled dreamily. "Brendan Crenshaw."

"Brendan. . ." she began, sure this was the beginning of a bad joke. "You mean, the same Brendan who was dating Marlene and Carlina?"

She rolled her eyes. "Well, he didn't really love them. It was only when we finally started dating that he understood what love was."

"And when did you two start dating?"

"I came home for winter break. Carlina decided to stay at school, so he was all alone. I called him up, we went out, and hit it off. We spent the entire break together. And so when it came time to go back to New Jersey, I couldn't." She smiled, "So I dropped out. And we've been together ever since."

"You know that he was with Carlina the night she died, though?"

"Of course," she said with a huff. "I told him to go. He was adamant that he didn't want to break things off with her via long-distance. He's considerate that way. So the day Carlina came back, he was going to break it off with her that night."

Mia blinked. This was new information. And it meant that the little jerk wasn't being completely honest with authorities. But who could blame him? His involvement with all these girls didn't exactly make him look good. "Do you know if he did? Were you in touch with him at all that night?"

"In touch with him? I was with him!" She laughed. "Carlina was always flighty and did things on a moment's notice without concern for anyone else. So, supposedly, they were all watching movies, and she just got up and left. Brendan said he was going to go out and look for her, but instead, he came to me. She was always doing things like that, treating him bad, and he was fed up with it. We were together until he got a text from Evvie saying she was still missing, and her mom didn't know where she was. Then he started to worry, so he went out to search for her. You can ask him."

Mia shook her head. "That's not necessary."

Blair shrugged. "So if you're looking for her killer, it's not me, and it's not Brendan. And obviously, it's not Coach Loos, since he died last week. If I were you, I'd check into Carlina's past."

"What past? What do you mean?"

A woman with an armload of clothes appeared between them, and they shuffled aside to let her pass into the dressing room. "I mean that

Brendan was *sure* Carlina was cheating on him. And Marlene, too." She lowered her voice, "*I think it might have been the same guy.*"

The mysterious D. "What makes you think that?"

"Because Marlene was beautiful and popular and the girl everyone wanted to be. Carlina, especially. So that's why she went after Brendan. And I think Marlene was dating this guy, Carlina found out about it, and so she set out to make the guy hers." She shrugged, "Carlina was pathetic. She hated all the attention Marlene got, even after her murder. So now, she gets to have the same attention. I hope she's happy."

"Do you know of anyone named D that Carlina might have been having a relationship with?"

Blair looked up at the ceiling, thinking. "D? No. I mean, there are a lot of Ds in our school, but I don't know of any . . . Sorry."

"It's all right," Mia said with a sigh. She looked down at the lace lingerie. Was that for Brendan? She guessed so. "Sorry to disturb your shopping trip. Thanks for the information."

Blair's face melted to a frown. "Maybe I'm forgetting someone. Maybe if you get a yearbook from the school, you can go through and find the D," she suggested. "Of course, it could just be a random person who has nothing to do with Oak Cliff High. In which case, I guess you're out of luck."

Mia nodded. It was a good idea; she'd try to find a yearbook, next. But if it was a random person? Yes. This would go down just as Marlene's case had—unsolved.

Mia wasn't ready to face that possibility just yet.

CHAPTER THIRTEEN

Sitting in the front of her car, sipping a coffee, Mia looked up from the copy of last year's Oak Cliff High School yearbook and frowned.

She'd been tearing through it, line after line, trying to find the name of another male student that might have been known as the infamous D, but though there were plenty, it was all just guesswork. There was a Scott Drummond in several club pictures with Carlina. A Dane Cowell who was in another photograph with Marlene. But there was nothing to say that they even knew each other. Perhaps, if she'd had one of the girl's yearbooks, with its signatures, she'd be able to tell if these boys knew Carlina or Marlene . . . but this was just a copy she'd gotten from the local library.

In other words, it proved nothing.

There was an entire memorial spread at the back of the book, for Marlene.

Taken from us too soon, it read. *Fly with the angels, sweet girl.* There were lots of photographs of her with Brendan, with the soccer team, with other girls, laughing and having fun. But nothing to give Mia any leads at all.

She flipped to the senior photograph of Carlina. It was the same one she'd seen on the piano at Carlina's house. "What secrets were you keeping?" she asked the photograph aloud. "Who is this mysterious D?"

She was so tired that she actually paused, as if hoping it would answer.

Then she shook her head, tossed the book aside, and drained the rest of her terrible, tepid coffee.

She looked around the park, shivering. It was empty. This was a good place to hide out. As she was leaving the shopping mall, she'd had another close call. A police officer had been parked outside the mall entrance.

For a moment, she'd thought that she was done for, that Evvie's mother had called the cops and given a description of her.

But the police had been picking up a shoplifter. Breathing a sigh of relief, she'd rushed to her car and zoomed away, making a promise to herself not to take any more risks.

Then, ten minutes later, she was at the Oak Cliff Library, stealing a yearbook.

Talk about risk.

But she couldn't apply for a library card because she couldn't give them ID. She couldn't stay there, either, because she couldn't stay *anywhere* for long without worrying that she was about to be caught. So she'd had to stick it under her sweatshirt and walk out, hoping no one noticed her. Thankfully, they hadn't.

Now, though, she felt like it was all for nothing. So much risk, no reward. She could've easily gotten caught at Evvie's house, or at the mall, or at the library.

She needed to dial back. Stay on the run. Stop meddling in this case.

Besides, she was no closer to finding Carlina's killer than she'd been when she first heard about the case. She should let David handle it.

David, the jerk who kept letting all her calls go right to voicemail.

And that was probably a good thing. He knew she was in too much danger. Now, he was trying to protect her.

She needed to protect herself. Go into hiding and forget this case.

Mia raised her hands over her head in a stretch, and when she looked down at her phone, she had a text from an unknown number. *It's DH. Meet me behind the old train station on Walnut at nine.*

David. The old train station. She knew that place because when they were working together, they'd get subs at a place down the street and park in the abandoned train station to eat and talk about the case. It was a good place to meet because it was surrounded by warehouses. No one would be there tonight.

A light sparked in her chest, and all of her thoughts of abandoning the case seemed to leave her. Maybe David had made more progress than she had.

She started up the car and headed off to the train station, thinking about what Evvie and Blair had said. This D person seemed like the missing link. If they just knew who it was, the case would be solved.

The old stone station had turrets and gorgeous architecture, though the roof was caving in and most of the windows had been blown out.

Though it was only eight-thirty when she arrived in the lot, David's car was already parked in front.

She pulled cautiously into the space next to him and looked over, checking to make sure he was alone. He gave her a wave.

She cut the ignition on her car, stepped out, and slid into the front passenger seat of his car.

"I hear you paid a visit to Evelyn Rhinehart," was his greeting.

She winced. "Not one of my smartest moves, I'll admit. So Mrs. Rhinehart called the police?"

He shook his head. "I went there to interview Evelyn and the mother insisted on seeing my badge and said some woman, impersonating an FBI agent, had been there earlier. I pieced it together."

"Ah." He handed her a coffee and a bag with a cinnamon roll in it, which she took. "Thanks. So, you learn anything?"

"Did you?"

She sighed and took a bite of the roll. "Not much. Well, I learned lots of things, but nothing that seems to bring us any closer to the killer. Did you happen to find any journals in Carlina's room? Under a floorboard?"

He shook his head. "Why?"

"Supposedly Evvie said Carlina was always writing in a journal. But she might have destroyed them because her mother was a snoop."

"The police have been all over that room. I'll tell them to do another check." He watched as she devoured the cinnamon roll, licking the sweet sugar off her fingers, and said, "You need anything?"

She nodded and looked away. "Well. . . I hate to ask . . . but . . ."

"Come on. What."

She blushed. "You have any money? I've only been able to rent hotel rooms with cash. I'm running low. I don't even have enough for a fleabag tonight."

He reached into his wallet and pulled out three twenties. "This is all I got. I can get you more, if you—"

"No. It's fine." She took them and stuffed them in her pocket. "Thanks. So what else did Evelyn tell you?"

"Not much. I know she's innocent. She and Fred were together and didn't leave her house until they went searching for Carlina. They were together the whole time. Did s'he mention someone named Blair to you?"

Mia nodded. "I checked her out. But she's clear, too. Turns out, she was with Brendan when the murder happened."

"Brendan? You sure? He told me he was wandering around town, alone. . . "

"Probably because he didn't want you finding out he was a total player. He cheated on Marlene with Carlina, and then, supposedly, he was cheating on Carlina with Blair, and according to Blair, he was supposed to break up with her, that night."

"Yeah? That's bad luck. Sounds like someone who wanted to get him in trouble. That's twice, now, he's been with the other woman when his real girlfriend's murdered? Hell."

She nodded. "I agree. But Brendan didn't mention having any enemies, did he?"

"Nope. He seemed like a likable enough guy. A little bit pampered by his parents, but not the murdering type. What about this D person? Did she know who that could be?"

Mia shook her head. "I went through the yearbook. There are some names, but nothing concrete. I think that person is the key. If we find D, we'll solve both murders."

"You think?"

She nodded. "Everyone seems to agree that Carlina was dating someone in secret. Brendan said he thought Marlene was also seeing someone else. Blair thinks it might've been the same person."

"Shit," he breathed, sipping his coffee. He winced, then, like there was something he had to tell her, but he didn't. They fell into silence, staring out into the black.

Finally, Mia broke it. "Yeah. So I don't know. Where do we go from here?"

David shook his head. "That's what I wanted to tell you. You don't go anywhere. I'm sorry, North, but you're being reckless. And for your own good, I need to--"

"Yes, but you're the one who called me in, needing my help—"

"I regret that."

She paused, at a loss for words. Did he really? "You do?"

"Yeah. I wanted your thoughts. Just thoughts. You see things in a unique way. I didn't mean for you to take over this investigation. I didn't want to put you in danger. But I should've known. You never let anything lie," he said, shaking his head. "You know how close you're coming to getting locked away, and them throwing away the key? Pretty damn close."

"Yes. Maybe. But you're the one who let the cat out of the bag, and it's not going back in. I need to see this through to the end."

"I get it. I know, that's in your blood."

"It is. And from now on, I'll be more careful. I'll—"

He waved a hand. "But think of what you're risking, Mia. If you want to see that husband and little girl of yours again . . . is it really worth it?"

She felt a quick stab in her heart.

He was right.

She dragged her hands down her face and stared out into the quiet night. "I guess."

"So that's what I came here to tell you. I came here to tell you thanks, but let me take care of it from now on. We've got some good leads, and we're following them. Including that D."

"You do?"

He nodded. "And yeah. You know I'm looking into your own case. But I can't really focus on it until I put this one to bed. We're close. So you can back away and let me wrap up these last details."

His words were encouraging, but he had a terrible poker face. He was just bluffing. He was probably just as lost as she was. Even so, his words were right. She was risking far too much. So she said, "All right. I'll stay out of it. If that's what you want. Have a good night."

She left her balled up napkin and full coffee in his car and stepped out.

"Take care of—" he started, but she slammed the door before he had a chance to finish.

When Mia got into her car, she backed out without looking back at him. Time to find another fleabag hotel with her sixty dollars. A hotel room, where she would sit, and do nothing at all, proving herself absolutely useless to everyone, a drain on society, like the criminal they thought she was. She'd promised.

*

This time, she drove far out of Dallas. She just kept driving south on 35 until she reached Temple, where she couldn't seem to keep her eyes open. She found an old motel on Stillhouse Hollow Lake. It was only forty-nine a night, leaving her enough change for an Egg McMuffin tomorrow, and, if she stuck with the dollar menu, maybe enough for lunch and dinner too. She checked in, yawning so much she could barely see straight. She climbed into bed the second she opened the door, and pulled the covers up to her chin.

She thought about some Sunday mornings, when she got to sleep in. Aiden would come and bring her a crossword puzzle book, hot coffee, and breakfast in bed, so that she felt like the most pampered woman on Earth.

Not anymore.

She looked around at her surroundings in the darkness. The hulking television set, the old fruitwood dresser, the drab flowered comforter, all illuminated by the glow of the VACANCY sign, blinking through the window. It was cold. Impersonal.

She dragged in a breath and let it out slowly, her lungs aching with the memories of the past. Everything was so wonderful, back then. Family, friends, home. She'd had it all. And yet she'd always been in such a rush to go out and do her job. She'd neglected it all.

With a heavy heart, she rolled over in bed, thinking of Kelsey. The little girl was turning into such a diva. Just shy of nine, and already spending hours in front of the mirror at home, getting ready.

Or did she?

Maybe she'd changed. She could have. Everything else in her life had changed so drastically. Maybe she didn't put any effort into her appearance.

A single tear escaped Mia's eye as she realized she didn't know her own daughter, anymore, at all.

Aiden had always been a great cook, but a messy one. Part of her life was going into the kitchen after he'd had his way with it, and cleaning up, closing every cabinet door and drawer that he'd left open. Was he still that messy? Or had he learned to change his ways, knowing that she was no longer there to clean up for him?

She'd been married to him for twelve years. And yet she didn't know him much, anymore, either.

She hadn't seen either of them for over two weeks.

That had to change. She'd told David she wouldn't take risks, but she couldn't not take this one. She had to go and see them again. Maybe not at their house, but somewhere. They had their rituals, like their Saturday morning jaunt to the wooden park in Crescent Lake.

Mia only hoped that they still kept them. She needed to see her family.

CHAPTER FOURTEEN

Mia drove to downtown Dallas in a thin drizzle. As she pulled up at the curb, she squinted past the raindrops on the windshield, and a shiver went down her spine. Fifty-nine Weston was beside an overgrown field, littered with discarded tires, rusting oil drums, the carcasses of long-expired automobiles and decaying railroad ties. There was a faded sign painted upon the brick façade of the building, over the door: *Fanciful Ribbon Company, EST 1912.* The front of the place was crisscrossed with graffiti-emblazoned wooden boards. No windows except for on the top floor, and those were dark. It looked like an abandoned warehouse below, some apartments on the second floor.

The back of her neck tingled. *I've been here before,* she thought. *This is a dream.*

She let her breath out slowly. She stepped out over a puddle, quickly crossed the sidewalk and pulled on the door handle, not expecting it to budge. To her surprise, it creaked open. She slipped it open a few inches and saw nothing but darkness.

She reached into her pocket and pulled out her cell phone to use as a flashlight. The building was an old manufacturing plant. The door entered into a small waiting room, with a spider-webbed receptionist's window, overlooking it. She treaded carefully across the peeling linoleum floor and opened the door opposite.

It led out to an expansive factory floor, full of hulking machinery from a bygone age. A gridwork of metal scaffolding hung several stories above, and the sheer size of the room made even the quiet, graceful steps of her shoes echo like a herd of thundering elephants. Pausing to listen, she heard only the sound of trickling water. Arcing the light from her phone across the expanse, she soon noticed the source of it. An enormous, swimming pool-sized puddle had formed in the center of the room, the result of a persistent leak from the ceiling above.

Mia shivered. The first time she'd done this, she'd felt like she was being watched.

Now, she was sure of it.

Her phone in her hand buzzed with a text. It was from David. *On my way. Be there in fifteen.*

Too late. He would be too late.

She looked down and footprints in the dust. Wet footprints. The prints headed off toward an opening to another room.

She already knew what she would find there. She told herself not to go, but it was like she couldn't help herself, like she was hovering above her body. She saw herself skirt the puddle, breaking into a run for the adjacent room. When she stopped abruptly, listening for any sound, she heard nothing but the steady drip of water.

"Hello?" she said, aloud this time, scanning the shapes of the machinery for any sign of life. "Ellis? Ellis Horvath?"

"*You*," a voice boomed in the darkness, cutting through the silence like a blade.

She froze and dropped her phone, sending a beam of light errantly swirling about like a disco ball. When it came to rest on the ground, it illuminated the man who'd spoken to her for the briefest of instances. He was sitting in a chair, in the very corner of the vast room.

Oh, God. RUN! A voice inside her screamed. But she was frozen, immobile.

By now, her eyes were adjusting to the minimal light. The man across the way was wearing glasses, his hair a little shaggy, but other than that, he was dressed in a business-casual way, with dockers and a button-down shirt. Good looking, respectable, and . . . someone she knew quite well.

It was Ellis Horvath.

He was holding something in his hand, half-obscured by shadows.

A gun?

No, it's not a gun! You're being set up! Get out of there.

She took a step backwards, reaching tentatively for her sidearm.

"Don't do it. Don't even move."

"Horvath?" she shouted, her voice echoing hollowly through the vast warehouse. "If you have Sara Waverly here, tell me where she is. No one has to get--"

"Don't talk, bitch."

His voice sounded strange. Harder than she remembered, almost otherworldly, like it was coming from everywhere, echoing around the entire expanse of the warehouse.

Suddenly, a gunshot went off, the sound, blasting her eardrums. She ducked instinctively. The sound seemed to ricochet wildly about the room, bouncing off walls around her.

She lunged forward to grab him, pulling him to the ground. He lifted his gun to her and fumbled on the trigger. Pushing his hand to the side, Mia fisted her hand around the handle of her gun and yanked it from her holster as she lost her grip on Ellis's arm. She hit the ground and aimed seconds later, firing off one round.

There came a sickeningly wet, guttural sound as her bullet found its mark. Grabbing her phone, she aimed the light at her target. A flower of bright red blood was blooming at his chest.

She stared at it, trying to comprehend, then looked at Horvath's eyes, which were rolling back into his head. She dipped a hand under his neck, feeling for a pulse, but there was nothing. His head lolled. He was still warm, but dead.

She'd killed him.

Suddenly, laughter echoed from all around her. She sat up, searching the shadows. There he was, standing, still, in the corner of the room.

He moved slightly forward, into the shaft of light.

It was . . .

Her eyes blinked open, and she found herself in the hotel room she'd only previously seen, the night before, in shadow. It was even grimmer in the light of day. The bedspread had yellow cigarette burn marks all over it, and the rust-colored carpet was worn down to threads, in places.

She rolled over and stared at a water-stained ceiling, thinking about her conversation with David. He was right that she needed to watch her own back and stay out of things, now that she'd given him her advice. He usually was. He'd always been her voice of reason.

With effort, she lifted herself from her bed and pulled on her jeans and hoodie. Then she got into her car and headed for University Park.

*

Crescent Lake Park, in the heart of University Park, had always been one of Mia's favorite places in the whole city.

When they were dating, she and Aiden used to come there, spread out a blanket on a knoll overlooking the lake, and have a picnic. A couple of times, they'd even come there after dark, when the place was closed, and made love there.

She'd have liked to think that it was during one of those times that Kelsey was conceived. She hadn't been planning to have children, since work was always so busy, but she wasn't getting any younger, either, so she decided to leave it in the hands of fate. And fate had provided that perfect little girl.

Both she and Aiden said all the time that they couldn't imagine a life without her. They'd even talked about having more, but fate hadn't provided that. Besides, she couldn't imagine how busy life would be with two. So they'd been happy, so happy, just the three of them. They'd fallen into routines. Donuts on Sunday mornings. Chinese on Wednesdays. Pizza on Friday. And Crescent Park on Saturday.

A year after Kelsey was born, the park administration announced plans to build a giant wooden castle on one of the knolls near the lake. A year later, it was complete, and since the park was already a favorite place for them to visit, Kelsey quickly declared that she was princess of that castle, and all the other kids who played there were her subjects. They'd stay there for hours, watching her explore the different wooden rooms of the massive castle, pushing her on the swings, just enjoying the sunny weather and the togetherness. Sometimes, they'd have a picnic on that same knoll overlooking the lake.

Now, as Mia pulled up to the vast gravel parking lot, it looked as though it might rain. She hoped that wouldn't keep them away.

But she needn't have worried, because the second she pulled into her spot, she saw her family's SUV, parked in the next row.

Her breath quickened as she raised her eyes to the structure, searching among the other park-goers for her family. There were a lot of kids, running in and out of the wooden doorways, slipping down the spiral slides, climbing the rungs and netting scattered about the castle, and going up and down on the big see-saws. Parents with strollers sat on the metal benches at the perimeter of the wood-chipped playground. Cries of childish glee erupted from the square.

Sure enough, Aiden and Kelsey were there, slightly away from the castle, on the regular swings.

Her heart double-timed. Had Kelsey grown? She looked tall, and even skinnier than before. Her hair had gotten longer, too—now it was nearly down to her tiny waist, and it flew out behind her like a kite's tail as she swung forward. She was wearing a brown, more mature jacket that Mia was sure she hadn't bought for her—had the old one with the hearts, the one she'd given to her for her last birthday, gotten too small, or did she think it was too babyish, now? Kelsey's mouth was open in great, big smile, so big that one would never know she had lived the past six months without her mother.

Mia cracked a window, hoping to hear some of her laughter. But she wasn't close enough.

She fought the urge to wave at them, to shout at them that she was there. Her lungs seemed to want that, just as much as her legs wanted to run to them and her arms wanted to hug them. Every part of her wanted them.

She put her hand on the car door handle, fighting with her brain, which was begging her to stay still. Things had been just as hard for them as they'd been for her. And they were in such a good mood, probably a rare one, considering everything they'd had to deal with.

Something prickled at the back of her neck, just as it had done during that dream, when she'd known she was being watched.

As much as every single part of her wanted to be with them, her brain finally won out.

As she powered up the window and prepared to pull away, her heart ached worse than ever. How unfair was it that she couldn't even wave at her own flesh and blood? That she could have no contact at all with the little girl who was starving for her mother's love?

I need to clear my name, she thought. *I need to see Wilson Andrews hang for what he's done.*

CHAPTER FIFTEEN

U.S. Marshal Kane Wilcox ran a hand through his scrubby white hair and cursed under his breath.

He could think of a thousand things he'd rather be doing this morning. One: he'd have loved to be one of those guys sitting on the edge of Crescent Lake, tossing in their lines. Fishing. When was the last time he'd gotten to do that?

Then there were the hundreds of other odd jobs his wife was waiting on him to do, back home. Thirty years of putting them off, because he always had to find his man, and now, no wonder Dana constantly grumbled to him. The place was practically falling apart.

Some days, he just wanted to cash it in, go home, succumb to retirement like all the other guys his age. Many of them had retired overseas, or to the beach, and had nothing more strenuous to do than chasing after grandkids.

Not that he had any of those. He and Dana had never had kids. They'd tried, but it wasn't in the cards.

And so as much as Dana wanted him home, making repairs to the house, whenever he asked her if he should retire, she always said, *What for? You're still young. And knowing you, you'd probably be bored within the first week.*

That was the truth. There was only so much fishing one could do. He loved his job, too. He was good at it. He always got his man, eventually.

And he was still young. Only fifty-four.

But there were parts of this job he didn't like. Sitting here. Waiting. Always waiting. He was a man of action. He needed to move.

As he watched a couple of boys working the monkey bars at the playground, their proud grandfather spotting them, he couldn't help but feel a twinge of longing. Raising a kid, teaching them everything they needed to know to succeed in life . . . he'd wanted to do that. And Dana would've made a great mom.

But, well . . . things didn't always work out.

He dragged his eyes away from the grandfather playing with his grandkids and forced them to where they needed to be—to the slim man in khakis and his pretty daughter, with the long, strawberry blonde spirals. They looked to be in the midst of a contest to see who could go higher on the swings. She chortled gleefully, and he shouted, "I'm going to get you! Watch this!"

"No!" she shouted back, laughing and pumping her long legs, driving herself even higher. "You can't beat that! My feet touched the sky!"

"All right, all right, you win," he laughed, slowing down.

Aiden and Kelsey North. They seemed to be doing quite well without Mia. But looks could be deceiving. It'd been a while since she'd been arrested for the murder of Ellis Horvath. Likely, they'd spent months in a fog, hoping this was a nightmare they'd soon wake up from.

Now, though, they were accepting this as the new normal. Finding happiness, even through the rain.

That's exactly what he and Dana had to do, after her last miscarriage, when it was determined they could never have kids.

Life goes on.

And life was going on for Mia, too, wherever she was. It was the reason he'd come here. He'd been parked down the street from the North house for the past few days, waiting for Mia to arrive.

He knew she would. He knew enough about her that she wouldn't try to keep away. But he'd been disappointed. She hadn't shown up. So when father and daughter piled into the car this Saturday morning, he'd had to follow. Maybe they were going to meet her in a secret location.

But no, they'd simply gone to the park to play.

Now, as they walked toward the see-saws, he threw his head back and groaned. This was another worthless outing. Maybe his hunch was wrong and Mia North had flown off to Mexico and was now sitting on a beach somewhere, slurping cocktails from a glass with a little umbrella.

Something he could be doing, too, if he just took that retirement package. But no . . . .

He yawned. Much more of this, and he'd fall asleep.

As he was about to grab his coffee from the cup holder and take a swig, he noticed her.

She was wearing a green hoodie and sunglasses despite the clouds, and standing by herself in the very corner of the playground. Watching them. A little curl of dark hair escaped from her tightly pulled hood. She looked around her, carefully, as if she was afraid of being found out.

"There you are . . .," he murmured, setting his coffee down and fumbling for the door handle. "Gotcha."

She began to walk toward her family who, oblivious to her, were bobbing up and down on the see-saw.

Kane jumped out of his car and bumped the door closed with his hip, then rushed across the green toward the castle structure. When he reached the wood-chipped surface of the playground, he pulled out his gun fluidly, leveling it at his target.

"U.S. Marshals! Freeze!" he shouted when he was about ten paces behind her.

The woman froze, as did everyone on the playground. Some people ducked and fell to the ground. Children began to shriek and cry. One shouted, "Mommy! That man has a gun!"

But the woman simply did as he asked and raised her hands above her head.

He kept his gun trained on the woman. "Turn around."

She didn't move.

"Turn around. Mia North. This is your last chance."

The woman began to spin, slowly. But the woman crumpled, crying. From here, he could now see that the woman had freckles. A different nose, pierced. Bright red lipstick. And she was younger, only in her early twenties. "Oh, my God. I'm sorry! I'm not Mia North! I'm just—"

"Mommy!" a little boy cried, rushing to the woman and grabbing her leg. "What's happening? Who is that crazy man?"

Kane lowered his gun. False alarm. "I'm sorry," he muttered. "Wrong person."

Shaking, she glared at him, then grabbed her son into her arms and hurried off.

Now, even more people on the playground were glaring daggers at him. Hands on his hips, he shifted his gaze to Aiden North, who'd gotten off the see-saw and was now staring at him with disgust.

"What the hell do you think you're doing?" he snapped, hugging his frightened daughter. "Were you following us?"

He shook his head and scanned the area, looking for Mia. He'd found the wrong target, but that didn't mean she wasn't here, somewhere. He could feel it. She was nearby. Somewhere.

"She's not here," Aiden North continued. "And you just ruined a bunch of kids' Saturday. You could've gotten a kid killed, drawing your gun like that in a public place. Good move, Agent."

He grabbed his daughter and the two of them headed back to the parking lot. The little girl Kelsey looked back at him, her eyes wide, as if to say, *You're not going to arrest my mom like that, are you?*

He didn't want to. But the law was the law. And her mother was a wanted woman.

Shaking his head, he holstered his gun and headed back the way he'd come. By then, the playground had cleared out.

Dammit, he thought to himself as he slid behind the wheel. *Well, that's just a perfect way to start my weekend. Maybe I should've taken that retirement. I could've spent today fishing.*

*

I knew it. I knew something was wrong.

Sunk down behind the wheel of her car in the parking lot, Mia watched the U.S. Marshal, a built, older man with a tough-as-nails sneer, holster his gun and head toward the parking lot opposite hers. He had a strut to him, an attitude, and she could tell by the way he'd pulled that gun on that poor mother that he wouldn't show any mercy to her, if he got her in the same situation.

She knew the Marshals would be after her. It was only a matter of time. She was an FBI agent, on the run, and the longer she evaded detection, the more they'd double down. They wouldn't simply forget that she was out there. She'd always figured the Feds would send one of their own to hunt her down, eventually.

But she hadn't known for sure that someone was after her until just now.

Now, she could put a face with the threat. A good thing, but then again . . . very bad.

He'd gotten close, this time. Too close.

If she'd obeyed her instincts and gone out to hug them, she'd be in the back of the Marshal's car right now, headed back to prison.

All the more reason to keep her head about her.

She shouldn't even be here. Watching them, even from a distance, was a risk.

She shook her head. David was right. She was being reckless, and she needed to stop.

She watched as the Marshal got into his car, then shifted her gaze toward Aiden and Kelsey. They were just a row away, a few cars over. So close. He'd sat Kelsey down on the bumper of their SUV and was leaning into her, smoothing her hair and whispering some comforting words. She couldn't hear, but she knew the gist: *Don't worry. Everything's all right.*

Kelsey was always full of questions. She was probably asking why that man was after her. What she'd done. Why he was so scary and tough-looking. Whether he would hurt her if he caught her.

Mia could just imagine her husband's response: *It's going to be fine. Your mother is tough, too. She can take care of herself.*

Kelsey shook her head and cried something in reply. Mia could imagine that, too: *Billy Sheridan says mom is an escaped convict and is going to fry when they catch her.*

Billy Sheridan, their next-door neighbor, was fond of feeding Kelsey the worst possible information to make her young imagination run wild.

But in this case, it wasn't exactly false.

Mia didn't know what would happen to her, if she was caught. In Texas, the Death Penalty was on the table, though rare. Maybe she wouldn't be fried, but she would be put away for a long, long time. Forget ever having a normal life with Kelsey, ever again.

At the SUV, Aiden scooped Kelsey into a hug and then helped her back into the car. She desperately wished she could climb into that car with them. That she could fall asleep in the passenger side, like she did, so many times, and not have a care in the world. That she could hand all her worries to her husband and let him take the wheel, for once.

But no. Aiden was a prince, but he couldn't help her, now. She had only herself to rely on. And she had to keep her wits about her.

I love you, she thought as she watched them pull out and drive away, wiping a tear from her eye. *But I don't think I can do this again.*

When she looked over at the Marshal's car, he was still there. Watching them leave. There was something raw and intense in his stare—a determination that made her pulse pound in her neck. She had a feeling he was the kind of person who didn't stop when he had a mission to fulfill. *Couldn't* stop.

Like her.

If he was after her, he'd stop at nothing to bring her in. And if she really wanted to be back with Aiden and Kelsey one day, she couldn't afford to make any more mistakes.

Swallowing, she started her car and pulled out of the parking spot. Then, taking one last look at her family, she stepped on the gas and made her way out of the lot.

CHAPTER SIXTEEN

Mia looked at the contents of her wallet and swallowed.

She had only nine dollars left.

Nine dollars, in her old life, had been nothing. She'd easily throw it away on a coffee and not even blink an eye. Now, it was all she had in the world.

She looked at the gas gauge on her car.

It was nearly on the E.

Pulling into the Texaco station, she filled the car with gas, making sure to stop the pump at nine exactly. That barely got it to the middle-mark on the gas gauge. The old car she'd lifted was good with gas, but not that good.

From now on, she wouldn't be able to travel far unless she came into some more money.

She was stuck.

She thought of that U.S. Marshal and shuddered. The city of Dallas was big, but not big enough. He'd find her. And soon.

As dusk descended, she pulled into a park on the edge of town. A sign on the entrance to the parking lot said OPEN DAWN TO DUSK. Even so, she considered sleeping there until she saw a police officer making the rounds in the lot, urging people to get a move on.

So she did, watching the gas gauge tick slowly down.

She passed a few empty parking lots and considered those. But the fact was, if she slept there tonight, she'd still be in the same predicament, the next day. Even worse, actually.

She needed help. Help from an unlikely source who didn't already have the possibility of a Fed surveilling them.

All at once, it came to her.

Nita.

Nita Franklin was a single mother whose husband had been killed in active duty in Afghanistan. She was doing the best she could to raise her nine-year-old daughter, Georgia, when the little girl opened up a window in her house, climbed out, and disappeared.

Because there were no signs of struggle and very few clues to her whereabouts, the police determined she'd run away and gave up hope of ever finding her. After all, thousands of children went missing every year, and that case had brought them nothing but dead ends.

But Mia had just had Kelsey, and it had opened up a whole new world to her. She hadn't known it was possible to love something so much. And she could just imagine how she'd feel if that thing was taken away from her. So she felt for Nita, and resolved to do everything possible to find the girl.

And she had. She'd interviewed everyone known to the girl. She'd even brough Kelsey with her on some of the interviews, breastfeeding her in the car. She hadn't stopped, working twenty-hour days to find the girl.

It had paid off. Four weeks after taking the case off the police's hand, she'd found a clue. Nita's brother, George, who Georgia was named after. Nita had thought she knew her brother inside and out. But it turned out, George had a dark side. He'd secretly been obsessed with his little niece. In an interview, Mia had been able to see the cracks in his calm façade. She'd excused herself to "use the bathroom," performed a cursory search, and found Georgia hidden in the closet of an upstairs bedroom in his condo.

She was unhurt, but frightened. And brother George had been given a ten-year prison sentence. Nita Franklin had been so grateful, she'd hugged Mia tight and said, "Thank you. I really thought she was gone forever. If there's ever anything I can do for you, please, don't hesitate to ask."

Now, as ashamed as she was to need to do it, it was time to collect on that offer.

She pulled up at the modest brick ranch, eyeing the place carefully. Did Nita and Georgia still live there? Gone was the old blue station wagon she remembered being in the driveway, the bright plastic sliding board and princess playhouse at the side of the home. But other than that, it was the same.

Checking over her shoulder—since she saw that U.S. Marshal, she couldn't stop doing that, now—she stepped out of the car and hurried up the front lawn, to the door. She rang the doorbell and looked around. A neighbor across the street was mowing his lawn. A couple of kids were playing basketball, down the street. Nobody seemed to be paying attention.

She let out the breath she'd been holding as the door swung open. It was Nita, though her hair was grayer, her dark skin more ashy, and she had a few more wrinkles around her eyes. She was wearing jeans and holding her place with her finger in a romance novel. She frowned. "Yes?"

"Hi, Nita. It's . . .," she faltered, not sure how to begin this awkward conversation. She pulled off her sunglasses and lowered her hood. "I don't know if you remember me. But—"

Her eyes went wide. "Oh, Mia! Mia North! It's you!" she said with excitement. She opened the screen door. "Please. Come in, come in."

"Thank you."

She stepped inside and looked around. The place hadn't changed much in the nine years since she'd been there. But there were a lot more photographs of Georgia. Mia found herself smiling at a graduation photo of the girl.

Nita beamed. "That's my Georgie. She'd have loved to see you, Mia. But she is away at college right now. She goes to Texas A&M. She's going to be a doctor."

"Really?" Mia managed a smile. "How wonderful."

"Yes, yes, she's so smart, she's getting straight As in all her classes," Nita said, ushering her toward the kitchen at the back of the house. "Sit, sit. Can I get you something to drink? I have lemonade."

Mia sat down. "That would be great, thanks."

The woman poured them both tall glasses, set one in front of Mia, and sat down beside her. "So, Mia, it's great to see you. I've been following your career closely over the years."

Mia's stomach lurched and she stiffened. "Then you know . . ."

"Yes. Of course," she said, her face falling. "You're a wanted criminal. I can't go a single day without seeing a bulletin on the television of a number to call if I see your face."

Mia swallowed, her body going tense as Nita glanced at the phone.

Was she going to call the police?

But then, Nita Franklin put a hand on Mia's. "But I don't believe a word of those things they say about you. I may have been wrong about my brother, but it taught me a thing or two about who is right, and who is wrong. And I know down in my soul that you couldn't have done the things you were accused of."

She gritted her teeth. "But I was *convicted* of them."

"And juries have never convicted the wrong person? Smoke and mirrors, I say," she said, shaking her head. "It's that awful man, Wilson Andrews. He smiles and he looks like a scarecrow. All fake inside."

Mia smiled sadly, relieved to have someone, finally, who didn't see her as a complete degenerate. "Thank you. I'm glad to hear you say that. If only others thought the same."

"What are you talking about? A lot of people think that way. They know he is nothing but a crook! And the minute I heard about it, I said to Georgie, mark my words, that scoundrel has a vendetta against our Mia and he's doing what he can to bury her." She shook her head. "Well, I don't believe that man will ever be senator. Mark my words."

Mia nodded. "It's true. I think he was looking for someone to frame for his brother's murders, and I was the easiest target. Because that Ellis Horvath had threatened my family."

She sighed. "Oh, that baby girl of yours! I pray for her every night. It must be hard without her momma."

Mia fisted her hands and steeled herself to keep from breaking down. "It's not easy, no." She looked around and said, "You do know that I escaped prison and that many people are trying to find me, to bring me in?"

"Yes. I'm so sorry, Mia. It is infuriating. You're one of the good ones. They treat you like this, after all you've done . . . ? It makes me spittin' mad."

"I appreciate that. I don't want to get you in trouble, so I shouldn't stay long, but I'm desperate, and —"

"Oh, child, what do you need? Money?" she said, standing up and going to a cookie jar near the sink. She pulled off the lid and reached inside, retrieving a stack of crumpled bills. "You can take all of this. I was saving it for a rainy day. And seeing you in such trouble seems like more of a thunderstorm."

She thrust the pile of money at Mia, who stared at it in amazement. Her heart swelled and tears came to her eyes, and for a moment, she was speechless with gratitude, but finally managed to swallow the lump in her throat and put the words together. "Oh, I can't take—"

"Please. I told you once, whatever I could do to repay the favor of bringing my Georgie back to me in one piece, I would do without question. You take this money and find a way to bring that Wilson Andrews down."

"Well, it's hard, considering I'm trying to evade capture."

“Yes, but these men, who abuse their power . . . they sicken me.” Now Nita was balling her hands into fists.

“Is everything all right?”

She shook her head. “It’s just a murder of one of Georgie’s classmates that occurred a couple days ago. It really has me on edge.”

Mia blinked. “Georgia knew Carlina Adams?”

Nita clutched at her heard. “Knew her? They were very good friends. She was friends with Marlene Dotts, too. The way a man could just prey on these girls like this . . .”

Mia stared at her, trying to comprehend. “I’m sorry. What man?”

“Well, of course it has to be a man, the way those girls were so brutally murdered. And a lot of us mothers have a good idea exactly who’s behind it.”

Mia leaned forward. “Who?”

“Peter Willington.”

“Peter . . .,” Mia said, running the name through her mind. The first name didn’t ring a bell, but the surname did. She’d heard the name batted around several times, over the years. “You don’t mean Edwin Willington? Dallas Mayor?”

She shook her head. “Peter. His son. He went to Oak Cliff High School with the girls. Graduated a couple years ahead, but he never made anything of himself. Got into drugs, abusing his daddy’s money.” She rolled her eyes. “Typical of a spoiled rich kid.”

“You think he was responsible for the deaths of Carlina and Marlene?”

She nodded. “More than just me! A lot of us think he’s responsible. He’s not all-there.” She touched the side of her head. “If you know what I mean.”

“No . . . what has he done?”

“Oh, it’s awful. I remember Georgie telling me that when he was in school with them, he used to sneak into the girl’s locker room and hide, and watch the girls as they changed.” She made a face. “He almost got expelled for that, but the mayor did his magic and got him readmitted. A week later, he locked a girl in one of the classrooms and assaulted her.”

“Oh, my gosh. And he never got in trouble for it?”

“A little slap on the wrist, is all. But when he graduated, he was up to no good, as well. He was never arrested, but there were always rumors floating around about him. He’d get into fights at bars, abuse women on the street. He'd spy on the girls in their homes. People noticed him lurking about and footprints outside their daughters' windows. I always made sure Georgie had her shades pulled down tight." She shook her head.

"You think this guy might have been targeting Marlene and Carlina?" Mia asked doubtfully. There'd been no mention of him at all, not from Brendan, Evvie, or Blair. And Peter wasn't a D-name. "Did he have any association with them, you think?"

She shrugged and went to a drawer, pulling out a news clipping. "I cut this out years ago, the first time it happened, to warn Georgie. Because despite his bad reputation, he was very popular among the ladies. I wanted her to make sure she stayed away from him. But maybe a lot of girls didn't."

Mia unfolded the yellowing bit of newsprint and read:

Questions Remain as to why Mayor's Son and Basketball Team Captain Peter Willington was Readmitted to OCHS after Lewd Incident

Oak Cliff—In October of this year, Dallas Mayor Edwin Willington's son, Peter, a sophomore, was discovered in the girl's locker room of Oak Cliff High School. According to multiple sources, females who were using the room at the time, Willington had been hiding in the locker room, indisposed, and had been propositioning girls for sex.

Mia scanned to a photograph of a young man who looked like a young Harrison Ford—right down to the knowing smirk. He was beyond handsome, with movie-star written all over him. "I see what you mean. He was charming, then?"

She nodded. "Very. Despite the weird situations he often found himself in. He has been terrorizing this town for years, and no one can do anything about it. Every charge against him gets swept under the rug and forgotten."

Mia made a mental note of the name. She read down a little farther on the article, her attention piqued by a single line: *Peter Willington, known as the Doughboy among teammates as a tongue-in-cheek reference to his tall, lanky frame, was a popular student at OCHS.*

Doughboy. D.

Suddenly, the idea that Peter Willington could have done this didn't seem so far-fetched.

"If it turns out he's a murderer, I'd hope those charges would stick." Even Jerry Andrews, with all his connections, couldn't escape prison for the murders he'd committed.

"I hope," Nita said, shaking her head. "Can I get you anything to eat?"

Mia stood up. "I don't think so. I appreciate it, though. Like I said, I inconvenienced you enough, and if word gets out I was here, you could be in a lot of trouble."

She waved her hand. "Oh, so what? My life's so boring since Georgie went off to school. I could probably use some excitement in my life!"

Mia smiled.

Nita went to the refrigerator and pulled out a few Tupperware containers of food. She stuffed them in a paper bag and handed them to Mia before she could argue. "This is my famous jambalaya and my chicken pot pie," she said with a smile. "Just heat them in the microwave for a couple of minutes each."

"Oh, but I—"

"Nonsense! Cooking for one is so hard. I always make extra," she said, patting her arm as she led her to the door. "You don't even have to return the dishes. I have plenty!"

She hugged the small woman when she reached the door. "Thank you so much," she said, sincerely. "I don't know how I can repay you."

"Remember, Mia? It's me, finally getting the chance to repay you. And anything more I can do, just ask." She shook her head. "I know how terrible it is, being away from my Georgie, and I see her almost every weekend. I can't imagine what you're going through with your little baby."

Mia felt a sob collecting in her throat, and stifled it. "Kelsey's almost nine. But she's what gives me the motivation to keep going every day. If it weren't for her and the hope that one day, I might be able to tuck her into bed at night, I might have given up. I will do it, one day. I know I will."

Nita rubbed her shoulder. "You poor thing."

Mia left with a wave. By the time she got outside, night had fallen and the kids and neighbor mowing the lawn had gone. She walked to her car, her spirits feeling a little lighter. Alone, on the run, it was easy to feel like the whole world was against her. But now she knew that wasn't so.

She slid into the front of her car and counted out the money. It was over six-hundred dollars. That would be enough for a while. Tonight she could get out of town, get a hotel room away from the heat, and eat a home-cooked meal.

That sounded nice. Of course, she'd have to repay Nita as soon as she could.

But what to do about Peter Willington? That was a solid lead. She could follow it, see if it panned out. She always followed her leads as far as she possibly could.

Then she thought about Kelsey. If she wanted that hope of tucking her daughter into bed to be a reality, she needed to stop being reckless, like David had said. She needed to stay in her lane and let him handle this case.

As she drove out of the Franklin's development, she picked up her burner phone and placed a call.

CHAPTER SEVENTEEN

David Hunter scowled as he looked over the faces of the men in blue, surrounding him. The FBI had taken over this investigation, but with the way the Dallas-Fort Worth Police department had been talking over him, all meeting, he was about to blow something up.

Lieutenant Gunther Briggs scratched his round belly and let out an obnoxious laugh from the head of the table. "Looks like even the FBI is stumped in this one, eh?" he said, giving David a slap on the arm. "You can't win all of them, you know."

The other officers smirked and laughed along with Briggs. David stiffened. "Like I said. There are a number of avenues we're actively pursuing."

"I get it. Right. Your D connection." He scoffed, "That narrows it down a lot. Hey, you're a D. Maybe *you* did it?"

He guffawed some more.

David calmly took a sip of his coffee, trying not to show a ripple. "All right. I've brought in all the leads we've looked into thus far. What do your guys have?"

He shrugged and motioned to the other officers. "Whole lot of nothin', right boys? In fact, the way this is looking, to me? I think our original supposition is correct. It's just a transient. And a coincidence that it happened to two girls from the same school. That's all."

"That's some coincidence," David pointed out.

Briggs shook his head. "It ain't if you consider we've been getting a lot of outsiders migrating this way. Murders are up thirty percent this year. All of 'em, committed by gang members or outsiders. And these girls aren't the gangbanging type. So we're back to outsiders. And that case, this Adams girl's murder's gonna go down in the books the same way Marlene's had. Unsolved."

"What about the journals? You find any journals in the floorboards?"

He nodded and picked up a red journal with a heart on it. "Yeah. Whole lot of nothing. A bunch of crushes she had in middle school, crap like that. Nothing revealing."

David grabbed the book and paged through it. Carlina's fat handwriting was that of a middle schooler. He read a part of it: *I think Brad L might like me cuz he keeps staring at me in Lit class ☺!*

He didn't have the stomach for much more.

This was it? There wasn't more? He shook his head and looked at the evidence they'd compiled. There were dozens of photographs of both crime scenes. Names of suspects. Snippets of interviews. *What would Mia do?* He wondered.

She sure as hell wouldn't give up. That much, he knew for sure.

"I'm going to go down to the school and do another sweep. See if anyone might know anything."

"Be my guest. It's a waste of time, if you ask me, though," Briggs said with a shrug. "We've been all over every inch of that school, questioning everyone who even looked at Carlina Adams. We even called up some of her classmates at that fancy college she went to. We ain't found nothing."

"Still. . ." His phone began to buzz. He looked at the display.

Mia.

Standing up, he headed for the door. "One second. I've got to take this."

He didn't pick up until he was standing outside the police station. Looking around, he answered with, "Yeah?"

"Hey," she said at once. "How's the investigation going?"

"It's going," he said doubtfully.

"That good, huh?"

"Pretty much dead. Briggs thinks it's the work of a transient."

"Of course he does. What an idiot. The crimes are nearly identical."

He chuckled. It was good to hear someone say what he was thinking, out loud. If Mia was here, they'd be able to commiserate over just what a douchebag Briggs was. He was the antithesis of everything Mia stood for. Lazy, incompetent, and self-important. The two of them had locked horns, more than once.

For a second, he felt guilty for giving her the boot, because right now, he felt like it was him against the world. He really could've used her on his side. "Exactly. That's what I tried to tell him."

"And the bull-headed ass didn't listen. Of course."

He laughed some more.

"Well, I might have a little lead for you."

He sighed. "Mia, I thought we discussed this, and you said . . ."

"I know. And I am. That's why I'm giving the lead to you and not tracking it down myself."

He frowned. "Where'd you get it from, then?"

"Never mind that. I think you should look into this name: Peter Willington."

"Willington . . . why does that sound familiar?"

"He's the mayor's son."

"The mayor's . . ." He dragged a hand down his face. This was opening a whole new can of worms. "Oh, shit. What did he do?"

"Well, he graduated a few years before the girls did, and he was a bit creepy. Had an incident where he was caught indisposed in the girl's locker room. Spying on them, I guess. And he's into drugs and has a bit of a rap sheet . . . you get the picture. He could be our man."

"But Peter. That's not a D—"

"He played basketball, and his nickname was The Doughboy. So he could be our guy. I know Brendan, Evvie, and Blair never mentioned him, but it's a possibility . . ."

David nodded. It was better than anything else they had to go on. "All right. I'll check into him." He paused. "You okay?"

"Yeah. Hanging in there. I've got to go. Good luck."

She ended the call without her normal send-off, which was, *I'll call you later to see what you found out.* He knew she cared. But maybe she was now realizing the danger she was in, and how much more important it was for her own well-being to stay hidden.

He couldn't blame her.

The best he could do for her, right now, was do as he promised and follow up on the lead. It wasn't like they had anything else to go on, anyway.

*

David Hunter wasn't too keen about tracking Peter Willington down at the mayor's mansion in the heart of the city. Luckily, though, he didn't have to worry about that. When he inputted the name into the FBI's database, he found the kid had his own condo in a high-rise on Victory Park Lane, a swanky section of mid-town Dallas known for its night-life.

When David arrived at the downstairs reception area, he didn't have to show his credentials. He said, "I'm here to see Peter Willing—"

"Yep." The man simply smirked and waved him on. "Go right up. Penthouse."

He stepped into the sleek glass elevator, along with a number of scantily-dressed twenty-something girls and guys in black, open-throated shirts that made the place smell like a Bath and Body Works. One of the girls said, in a throaty voice, "I can't wait to get effing toasted," and another guy said, "Well, Dough's always good for that."

Great. So the kid was having a rager. It made sense. It was ten o'clock on a Saturday night.

When the elevator doors opened, the place smelled like pot. He walked out, following the party-goers, feeling like he'd walked into a Bret Easton Ellis novel.

The penthouse's living space was the size of a basketball court, with high ceilings and windows overlooking all of Dallas. There were white sofas everywhere and chrome fixtures, everything very plain. What wasn't plain were the many bodies, packed into the space. Loud music was pumping, and bodies writhed under the bright white lights.

A young girl flung herself into his arms. "Hey," she slurred, kissing him full on the lips. She tasted of alcohol.

Drunk. He politely nudged her aside and saw a couple of kids snorting lines of coke from a coffee table. *And worse. Shit. How old are these kids?*

If he'd been here to make arrests, there were about two-hundred candidates for that, right here in this room. But he tore his gaze from the sight of two girls, making out on a sofa, and stepped toward a guy who looked somewhat sober, bopping along to the music and sipping a beer from the corner of the fray.

"Hey. Where's Peter Willington?"

The guy looked him over. "Who's asking, old man?"

David stiffened. *So thirty-five qualifies as old? I bet I could bench press twice what you can,* he thought. He pulled out his credentials and flashed them.

The kid's eyes went wide. "Shit. That's real?"

He nodded.

Gnawing on his lip, he pointed down the hallway. "First room on the right."

He pushed past the kid, who he could immediately sense was whispering to others behind his back, *He's a Fed!* As he reached the hallway and the music faded behind him, he knocked on the door and braced himself, wondering if he'd find this kid in bed, indisposed, with a girl.

"Come on in!" a voice called.

The doors were made of light paper screens, like that in a Japanese dojo. He slid it open and a wall of hot steam hit him.

No, he needn't have worried that Peter was with *a* girl. The kid was with half a dozen girls. They were in a giant hot tub, the girls sandwiching the tall boy, who was wearing sunglasses and smoking a joint. He was trying to reach his arms around as many of them as possible.

As David neared, he realized they were all *sans* clothing.

He looked up as David approached him. "Hey. I don't know you. But it's all good. Hop in. I can't handle all these on my own."

David flipped him his credentials.

He pulled off his sunglasses, squinted at it, and smirked. "A Fed, huh? Nice." He accepted a kiss from one of the girls next to him and said, "Offer still stands."

David frowned. "I'm here to question you about the murder of Carlina Adams."

That finally produced the desired result. The smile faded. He sucked in another drag of his joint, stubbed it out, and snapped his fingers. "Girls. I've got to go. Keep my spot warm for me. Okay?"

He lifted himself up out of the hot tub. Sure enough, he was completely naked. Grabbing a towel, he slung it around his waist and strutted for the door. "Come on, Agent. Let's go get a drink somewhere quiet."

He followed him outside, to a patio overlooking the city. Peter went behind the bar and smiled.

"What's your poison, Agent . . ."

"Hunter. And if I'm not mistaken, you're too young to drink."

A slow, easy grin appeared on his face. "That's right." He reached for a liter of soda and poured them each a glass. "Happy?"

David didn't reach for it. "Yeah. So you knew Carlina?"

He nodded. "Yeah. Hot little piece, she was. And before you go asking, I knew Marlene, too." He smacked his lips. "They were both really good, if you know what I mean."

"No, I don't," he said, even though he did. He didn't want to think he had anything in common with this dirtbag. He fought to keep his lip from curling in disgust. "So you had a relationship with them?"

He chuckled, took a sip of his soda, and stared out at the flickering city lights below. “I don’t do relationships. Not my style.”

“You graduated before they did, right?”

He nodded. “A year before. Yeah.”

“When was the last time you saw them?”

He shrugged. “Don’t know. I see a lot of girls, Agent. No one special. You know how it is.”

“What about getting expelled from school. How did that happen?”

Behind David, the door slid open, and a girl with bleary eyes, wearing nothing but a towel, poked her head out.

“There you are, Michael!” She crossed over to him and threw herself at him. The two began to make out in earnest.

David started to turn away, disgusted, when something struck him. “Michael? I thought you were—”

He chuckled and extended his hand as the woman clung to his neck, sucking on it. “Michael Willington. If you’re looking for the guy who was expelled? That was Peter. My twin brother.”

Shit. The guy was jerking him around. David didn’t take his hand. “And where’s he?”

He smirked. “No clue. He left a couple days ago. Haven’t seen him since.”

“A couple days ago . . . when?”

“I don’t know. Wednesday?”

Wednesday. So the night that Carlina was murdered.

“Does he do that often?”

Michael wrapped his arms around the girl, who was now glaring at David like he was interrupting something. “Yep. All the time. Dough’s got a couple screws loose. He goes off like this all the time.”

The girl nodded in agreement. “He’s intense,” she whispered.

“And the reason he was nearly expelled, a couple years ago?” David asked.

The girl giggled. “Oh, my God, what didn’t he do? He used to peek in my windows while I was changing! Vivian caught him jerking off behind the bleachers once while we were at cheerleading practice. He’s a creeper. Everyone knows it.”

Michael nibbled on her throat. “Yeah, ain’t that the truth?”

David gritted his teeth. Mia’s lead was sounding more and more credible, and yet still so far away. “And you don’t know where he could be?”

He shrugged and pulled the girl in for a kiss.

"No place of work? Places he liked to hang out?"

"Work?" He threw his head back and laughed. "You really think we work? That's for suckers."

"Okay . . . but you have to have some idea?"

"Nope, none. Could be anywhere, really," Michael murmured. It sounded like a cover for his brother, but by then he was making out in earnest with the girl, and David really couldn't take any more of it.

He turned and went out the way he'd come. By the time he reached the living room, it had quieted down considerably. The music was still pumping, but every eye in the place was on him, watching him as he made his exit.

News had traveled fast. He was the official buzzkill.

But now he really had to find Peter Willington. If he was the killer, and he'd murdered Carlina, that meant he could be stalking another victim. He just didn't know.

CHAPTER EIGHTEEN

Evvie Rhinehart ran some gel through her short blonde hair and stuck new dangly earrings into all of her ear holes. Standing back and inspecting her make-up in the mirror, she smiled.

"Looking good," she whispered.

She'd always been the wallflower, the quiet one in the group. The girl none of the guys ever seemed to notice.

But now, that was about to change.

Her heart leapt as she glanced at the message she'd received from Brendan: *Hey. You busy.*

Taking a deep breath, she typed in: *No. What do you need?*

She'd thought, at first, that Brendan had just wanted to get photos from her for the memorial and vigil they were organizing at the high school. Of course, that had to be it.

But then he replied: *Just thought you might want to get together and talk. Just the two of us.*

Of course, it made sense. Carlina was the closest to both of them. They could bond over their mutual grief for her.

But then she typed in: *Sure, when?*

And he responded with: *How about now?*

It was late at night, almost eleven, and she was home alone. It wasn't exactly a great time for getting together and mourning a mutual friend. She typed in: *Well, my parents aren't home. They went away for the weekend.*

His response was almost instant: *Perfect.*

So that meant . . . what did that mean?

He was coming to her house, at night, and there'd be no parental supervision. Her heart fluttered at the thought of it.

Brendan Crenshaw. Decorated quarterback. President of her high school class. Homecoming king. All-around most popular kid of her high school class.

He wanted to see her.

Sure, it was a year later, and all those high school designations didn't matter. It didn't matter that he'd been the most popular guy in their class, any more than it mattered that she'd been the shy class bookworm, better known as the Best Friend of Carlina Adams.

Now, he was coming to see her.

But he was still Carlina Adams's boyfriend. Her death didn't mean anything. He had to express his devotion to her, right? She wasn't even in the ground yet. He had to show his respect. That's probably what this was. He wanted to reminisce about Carlina, talk out his feelings.

She was good at that. The shoulder to cry on. The person who listened. Even in her yearbook, most people had written, *You're such a great listener!*

A great listener. That was just . . . freaking wonderful.

No, she wasn't a talented quarterback or a beautiful woman or a star soccer player.

She had a great ear. The end.

Of course, that's what Brendan wanted her for. Her stupid ear.

That's probably why Carlina had always shared so much about her life with Evvie. She had a life, and Evvie, well, didn't. Aside from a few awkward, sloppy kisses with Fred, her sex life was nil. When she'd said to Carlina, "I don't understand why you hate Brendan! He's like the perfect guy," she'd replied, "Oh, Evvie, don't be so naïve. He's nice and all, but I've had far better sex in my life." And she'd done that mysterious wink thing.

Was Brendan that bad in bed? And who had she been having all this sex with? As far as Evvie knew, Brendan had been Carlina's first serious boyfriend.

Ugh. She was doing it again. Overthinking things. Mrs. Prescott, her guidance counselor, always told her that overthinking got her into trouble.

And that was just what she was doing, now. Imagining Brendan, on top of her . . .

Stop, Evvie. Remember what Prescott says. Take a step back. Breathe. Don't overthink, but don't react too quickly, either. Your first reaction isn't the best one. Usually, your second one is.

She glanced at the mirror again and straightened her sweater. Her second reaction?

Pretty fine. She turned in profile, wondering if it made her look anything like Carlina. Carlina, who was gorgeous and feminine and well-endowed. Who most of the guys at school drooled over. Who was mean, most of the time, and yet people gave her a free pass because she was just so angelic-looking. Who'd treated Brendan like crap, all those months she was with him. Meanwhile, Evvie had dated slow, dim-witted, goofy Fred, *wishing* she could have a boyfriend as hot and as appealing as Brendan.

Of course, Carlina was her best friend. So she'd never said a thing. All those years, ever since Freshman year, she'd lusted after Brendan, his form filling her nighttime fantasies . . . and yet, she'd never told a soul. She'd spent so many days and nights in his circle of friends, watched him go on from Marlene, to Carlina, and never said a word.

Now, though. . . did it matter? Carlina was gone. Marlene was gone. And she and Brendan were still here. In a way, it only made sense.

She glanced down at his message and smiled. Then she texted: *How soon can you get here?*

He responded with: *Five minutes. I'm just around the corner.*

Just around the corner? Had he been thinking about her, too? A thrill skittered its way up her spine. She imagined Brendan, in front of her. Kissing him. She could barely think straight. Kissing Brendan Crenshaw? Her hands shook.

Her first reaction was to freak out. Her second one, too.

Thanks, Mrs. Prescott.

She needed to calm herself down.

Turning off the light to her bedroom, she'd just begun to spin toward the front door when she saw it.

A face in her bedroom window.

She gasped. It was there, pale as moonlight, leering at her. A man.

Quickly, she swung back, searching out the face in the darkness. It was a flash of a thing, there and then gone. Turning on the light, she swallowed. All she saw in the window frame was utter blackness.

A fierce wind shook the house. She stepped closer to the window, inching her way across the bedroom, the floorboards underneath her, creaking. When she reached the window, she peered out the screen. Nothing. Lifting the screen, she carefully stuck her head out, expecting to see someone running for cover.

Searching the darkness, she saw something rustling in the woods at the side of the house. A person? The wind? An animal?

"Hey!" she shouted, shivers traveling the length of her spine. Had it been the murderer? Her imagination? Or . . .

Suddenly, a thought came to her. The creeper.

It'd been a long time since she thought of him. That guy, Peter. He'd gone to her high school, he and his twin brother Michael. The mayor's sons. It'd been a couple of years ago since she'd heard about him, but he was fond of peeking in people's windows, all over town. What had ever happened to him? Was he back?

Shrugging off the thought, she closed the window tight, pulling the shade down. One never could be too careful.

A moment later, she heard a car, pulling up in front of her house. The brakes squealed and she heard the door open, and slam shut.

Brendan. He was here.

For her, this time, and not for Carlina. All those times, he'd sat in her house, cuddled up with Carlina as they watched movies. Carlina had always gazed at her like, *Ugh, I wish this guy would give me my space!* Meanwhile, Evvie had wished she could be closer to him. In his arms, feeling them around her.

She took a deep breath, just as Mrs. Prescott had advised. This time, it helped.

She all but skipped toward the front door. She opened it, just as Brendan was stepping to the porch. His hair was mussed and his eyes were rimmed in red, but he couldn't possibly look bad. In fact, the flaws made him look more beautiful than ever. "Hi."

"Hey." His voice was a low, sexy rumble. "What's wrong?"

"Uh . . . you remember that guy? The creeper?"

He looked surprised. "Doughboy?" He shrugged. "Haven't seen him around. Why?"

"I just . . . oh—nothing." She opened the screen door for him and let him in, and a rush of awkwardness fell over her. "Uh. Like I said, my parents aren't home. And I really shouldn't be having anyone over."

"Do you always do what your parents tell you to?"

She laughed, "Not always."

"Good." He took off his jacket and threw it on the ground, gazing at her.

The gaze was so intense, she had to look away, and started to babble. "Uh. Her parents said her funeral's going to be on Monday. Are you going?"

"Evvie."

Her name, on his lips, was so startling, she couldn't help but look back at him.

There was something on his face she couldn't quite understand. He looked troubled, as if there was a war going on in his head. He raked his hands through his hair and said, "I don't really want to talk about her."

Good, she thought, her heart skipping madly. "Then what do you want to talk about?"

He shook his head. "Nothing really. I don't really want to talk at all."

"Okay. Then . . ." She let out a nervous laugh.

Before she could finish. he bridged the distance between them, captured her face in his hands, and lowered his mouth onto hers.

CHAPTER NINETEEN

The first thing Mia did when she woke up in the pre-dawn hours of morning was grab her phone off the night table and check the news.

She thought for sure there'd be some breaking news about how an arrest had been made in the murder of Carlina Adams. A Peter Willington, the unstable mayor's son.

But there was nothing. The most recent article was from the day before: *Police, FBI, looking for leads in case of murdered teen.*

She sighed. Then she sat up in bed and looked around. She couldn't remember what town she'd eventually stopped in, but it was south of Dallas. Not a terrible place, either—this hotel room was neat and tidy. Not that she'd ever be able to stay here again. No, that was too dangerous.

She quickly changed and went outside, finding herself in a wooded area, by a long, pretty lake. The parking lot of the motel was deserted. She wandered down to the water's edge and checked her phone. It was only six.

Oh, well. Time for David to wake up.

She was surprised how alert he sounded when he answered. "Hey, North."

"You're up?"

"Been up all night."

"So . . . Peter?"

"Working on it. Hell, the night I had last night? You wouldn't believe."

She perched on a park bench, already wishing she could've been there. "What happened?"

"I went to this really swanky condo that Peter lives at with his twin brother, Michael."

"He has a twin? I didn't know that."

"I didn't, either, until I got there. Anyway, Michael was there, and that kid's a piece of work. He's—what? Nineteen? And living the Hollywood life—drugs, girls, parties. He was stoned and in a hot tub with a bunch of girls when I found him. Mayor Willington must be so proud."

"And Peter?"

"Wasn't there. They hadn't seen him since the night Carlina was killed. But they confirmed he was a pretty creepy, weird guy. Liked to stalk the girls. So it looks like a solid lead."

"Do you have any idea where he could be?"

"A little bit of one. Michael seemed to think he didn't work, but I looked into it and found he had an employment record for a hobby shop in the South Street Mall in Waco. So I thought I'd check into it this afternoon. Place doesn't open until ten, and I've got to meet with Briggs at ten, unfortunately."

The South Street Mall. Mia looked around. She couldn't have been too far away from Waco. And a mall was big, far from the city of Dallas. Fewer people were probably looking for her, there. It could be safe . . .

And if Peter was really the killer . . .

She could end this. Today.

"What about the journals in Carlina's room? Did anyone find anything?"

"Yeah. Just one. It was all hearts and flowers. From middle school. Nothing earth-shattering."

"Really? Did you search the whole room?"

"Police did. They said they were pretty thorough. Maybe she burned the other ones, like she said. I'll give it another look, when I have a chance."

"Okay, well, let me know what you find," she said, and hung up.

She sat there for a few moments, twiddling her thumbs. Then she stood up to get her things and get on the road. She really didn't have anything else to do. A trip to a mall in Waco, to do some window-shopping, wouldn't kill her.

*

It turned out that the mall was only fifteen minutes from the motel. It seemed like fate was demanding that she go.

She got there early, and spied *Calico Comics,* the only comics store in the sprawling, two-story building full of hundreds of stores. Sure enough, the entrance was blocked by a roll-up metal gate. A sign in the window, emblazoned with Spiderman and Wolverine, announced that it opened at ten.

She went to the food court, which was just across from the comics shop. The only fast-food place open was a little coffee shop. She ordered a coffee and donut from the pretty girl at the counter and decided to sit, right across from the shop, where she could see anyone going in or out.

As the girl handed Mia her change, Mia said, "Can I ask you a question? You must see a lot of what goes on in this mall. Do you know anyone who works in that comics store?"

The girl giggled at the tall boy working with her and said, "Yeah. We were just talking about that. They're so weird."

"Are they?"

"Yeah. They're stalkers. Every one of them. *So* weird."

"Have you spoken to them?"

She groaned. "Unfortunately. They come here and sit and watch the girls and guys. One of them asked me out. Like I'd do that."

"Which one?"

She shrugged. "I don't know his name." She looked past Mia and her eyes widened. She whispered, "Speaking of, here comes one now. Ugh. He's going to come and order a white cream donut and sit there and watch me, the whole time!"

The poor girl looked rattled as the guy working with her said, "I'll take care of it. You go in the back."

She smiled gratefully at him and hurried through the door.

Mia quickly grabbed her bag and coffee and stepped aside. As she did, a short, fat kid in a t-shirt and jeans came up behind her and said, voice cracking, "White cream donut please."

Mia looked back at him. The unfortunate kid had more acne on his face than she'd ever seen, and his nose was running. But it wasn't Peter. Peter had played on the basketball team. He was handsome.

As he collected his donut and placed his money down, Mia said, "Do you work with someone named Peter?"

The kid looked at her, seemingly shocked that someone would try to talk to him. "What?"

"Peter Willington."

He cleared his throat. "I don't know. Leave me alone."

And he scurried away, eyeing her like *she* was the stalker.

Well, she was a wanted criminal, and that was probably worse. She couldn't afford to call attention to herself.

She was about to turn away when the boy said, "Willington? I know him."

She turned her full attention to the kid. "You do?"

"Yeah. Sure. He works at the comics store. But right now, he's probably down on floor one."

"How do you know?"

He laughed. "Because he always comes in early. He watches the girls opening up at the lingerie shop." He circled a finger by his head. "A little crazy, that guy. He's good-looking. He could probably get all the tail he wants, if he just acted normal. But he can't seem to do it. He's got this nervous tic and a few screws loose. Scares all the girls off."

That was interesting. "Downstairs, you said?"

He nodded and pointed to the escalator.

"Thanks."

Grabbing the bag with her breakfast tight in her fist, she headed for the escalator. When she stepped on it and was halfway down, she saw him. The place was pretty empty, but there was a lanky kid, sitting on a bench across from Lovely Ladies Lingerie, elbows on his knees, watching the display window like a coach watches a game.

Mia took the escalator the rest of the way and hurried behind the giant planter that ran through the middle of the walkway. She moved behind him, watching. Sure enough, he was gazing at a girl who was dressing a mannequin. The girl was trying to ignore him, but every so often she'd glance back at him and scowl.

So interested was Peter in this girl that he never noticed Mia, watching him from behind.

Of course he's the killer. He's a creep. He has a D nickname. And the only reason no one has suspected him is because his father is Mayor, Mia thought, moving closer to him.

He shifted a little, reaching for his crotch, and for a moment, she thought he might try to unzip his pants and expose himself.

Before he could, she stepped in front of him and said, "Peter Willington?"

His eyes shifted to hers, and a frown appeared on his face. "Who are you?"

"I'm an investigator. I have some questions to ask you about the murder of Carlina Adams?"

He rose to his full height, at least a foot taller than Mia, and stared her down. "Who? Sorry, I've got to go."

He nudged her aside and started to walk away.

"Wait," she said, following him. "You had to have known Carlina. She went to school with you. She was murdered a few days ago."

He glanced at her. "I don't know her."

"You knew Marlene Dotts?"

He shook his head again. "I don't know anything. I graduated two years ago. I don't pay attention to school drama." He started to pick up the pace. "Leave me alone."

She stopped and called after him. "Was it true that you were stalking girls in the high school locker room?"

He froze. Turned. "That was a story my ex made up. Yeah, I followed her into the locker room. But she made up all this bullshit. It wasn't true. I'm no stalker."

"What were you doing just now?"

He pressed his lips together. "Nothing. I just—forget it."

He tried to turn, but she blurted another question. "Where were you on Wednesday, when Carlina was murdered?"

He blinked. "I don't—home, I guess."

"Your brother Michael said you left Wednesday night and he hasn't seen you since."

He let out a breath. "Who are you? A cop? You can't touch me, then. Besides, I didn't do anything wrong. Leave me alone."

"I'm not a cop," she said, following him as he took a quick right down a narrow hallway toward an EXIT sign. "And I want answers."

He whirled and suddenly advanced on her. "You're not, are you?"

She realized that here she was, in a narrow hallway, alone with a man who could be a murderer. And she was unarmed. "Tell me why you killed Carlina."

His scowl suddenly gave way to a smile. "You'll stop at nothing, huh?" He moved forward another step, backing her up against the wall. "I didn't kill her. But I'll tell you what I want to do to her. What I want to do to all women. I want to push them up against a wall and pound them so hard that they can't ever walk again. So they can't even breathe."

Her breath quickened. He moved so close to her, his warm breath in his face, his eyes the only thing she could see. He ran a cold fingertip down her cheek.

"Is that what you want?" he said with a smile.

She shook her head, almost imperceptibly.

"Fortunately for you, I have some self-control," he said pushing away from her. "Then again, you might be asking for it."

He started to move for her again, but in a split second, she swung a wild hand out, knocking him on the side of the head. His eyes went wide in shock and his lips curled in rage as he began to curl his fingers into a fist.

"You stupid—"

She punched him again, this time, with her own fist, as hard as she could. He slammed up against the wall, his skull ricocheting off the hard surface. Then, he seemed to hang there in mid-air for a moment, before sliding to the ground along the wall and falling over, unconscious.

Mia stood there, at his feet, breathing hard. Crouching, she checked his pulse.

She looked up and down the hallway. It was empty.

Quickly, she rose to her feet and tore for the door at the end of the hall, marked EXIT.

She quickly punched in a text to David: *Saw him at the mall. He attacked me. He's in the service hallway on the first floor, next to the lingerie shop.*

And she ran to her car, got in, and drove as fast as she could, away from the mall.

CHAPTER TWENTY

Evvie rolled over in bed and looked at the sleeping form next to her.

Her heart fluttered wildly again.

Brendan Crenshaw was in her bed. Her bed. Her bed.

He was in her bed!

Her breath hitched and she stifled a yelp of excitement.

She hadn't slept at all last night, not just because of their lovemaking—could it be called that?— but because he was here. Carlina had told her that sex with Brendan was nothing to write home about, but Evvie felt like she could write a novel. Not that she knew much—or anything—about sex. She knew a lot about groping—Fred seemed fond of doing that, grabbing blindly under her clothes after he'd had a couple too many beers at a party, squeezing her boobs like he was milking a cow.

But this? Her first time? It had been everything she'd hoped for. Almost like a scene from a movie. He'd lifted her up, carried her to the bed, stripped her down and told her she was beautiful. And when he'd entered her, he'd kept his eyes locked on hers. "This okay?" he'd asked her, gently, as if he wanted to make things right for her.

Her stomach fluttered again.

She stared at him, taking in his long eyelashes, the manly stubble dotting the curve of his jaw, his pink pillowy lips, the arch of his eyebrows. He was gorgeous, even after the crazy night they'd had. She couldn't take her eyes off him.

And now, they were together. A couple. Screw Fred. He'd always been so ambivalent, anyway. Unlike Brendan, a real man, who came in and took what he wanted.

She smiled at the thought of him, barreling into her house like John Wayne in *A Quiet Man,* grabbing her like a startled Maureen O'Hara and pulling her to him, kissing her for all he was worth. So romantic. So passionate. So brave.

That was a real man. That was Brendan.

His eyes fluttered, and he cracked one open. Then he looked around, a little confused, as if he'd forgotten where he'd gone to bed last night. Maybe she'd done that to him—loved him so silly, he'd forgotten everything but her.

"Hey," he said, stretching his arms over his head. "What time is it?"

"Ten." She leaned in to kiss his jaw, but he suddenly popped up.

"Oh, shit," he said, rubbing an eye. "I've got to get home."

"You do?"

He snaked an arm around her under the sheets. "Why? Want to go again?"

A high-pitch giggle erupted from her lips. Since when did she giggle? Brendan just had that effect on her. She wouldn't have minded it, but in the light of day, she felt self-conscious. "It's okay. I have a lunch date, anyway."

His eyes narrowed. "Lunch date? You tryna make me jealous?"

She giggled again. Was he jealous? "No. It's with Prescott."

"Prescott?" He laughed. "You mean, the guidance counselor from high school? That Prescott?"

She nodded, a little embarrassed. Judging from the reaction she'd gotten from Carlina, hanging out with one's old teachers wasn't a cool thing to do.

"Why do you hang out with her? You still need her guidance? You graduated last year."

"I know. But she's nice. We get along really well. So we go out to lunch every other Sunday."

"That's . . . weird. But okay. Whatever." He rolled over and got out of bed, then pulled on his boxer briefs and jeans. "Have you been talking to the police at all?"

"Yeah." She rolled her eyes. "I'm getting interviewed so much, I feel famous. The police, the FBI . . . even this woman who claimed to be from the FBI. I think she was a reporter or something. They've all been asking about--"

"What have you been telling them?" he said, his face suddenly serious.

"Oh. You know. Nothing much. Just the truth."

"What truth?"

She let out a short laugh. "I thought there's only one version of the truth."

"No. Everyone has their own version of the truth. What's yours?"

He suddenly sounded suspicious. She wondered if she'd upset him. "I don't know. Just that we were together, the four of us, and that she left to put up her windows."

"And?"

"And I guess it's not what they want to hear. They seem to think Carlina told me everything about her life."

"Did she?"

Evvie shook her head. "She told me most things. She was my best friend. But she didn't tell me everything."

His lips twisted. "She was seeing some other guy, wasn't she?"

Evvie shrugged. "I don't know. I think so."

He let out a sigh. "I got that feeling, too. She never gave you any idea who?"

"Nope. I think the police wanted that information, too. They said it was someone named D. But who could that be?"

"D?" He frowned. "No clue." He snapped his fingers. "Donovan?"

She giggled. "Really?"

"Yeah, I know. But he's the only guy I know of with a D name."

"He's a science teacher. And he's also a total dork." She giggled. "He looks so hot in those safety goggles!"

Brendan laughed, pulled on his shirt, and leaned over to kiss her. This time, it was a chaste one, on the forehead. "Uh . . . I'll see you."

"When?" she asked, breathless, and was immediately embarrassed at how needy she sounded.

"I don't know. I'll text you." He scuffed into his sneakers and opened the door, then turned back. "Hey. You probably shouldn't tell the FBI or the police about this. About us. Okay?"

"Why?"

"Well, you know. Marlene. And Carlina . . . it just doesn't look great for me."

She wrapped a sheet around herself and followed him to the door. "Sure. I get it."

She stood behind him as he opened the front door, hoping he'd turn and give her a goodbye kiss, there. But he didn't. He simply waved, tossed a "See you later" over his shoulder, and headed across the lawn to his car.

She watched him drive away and sighed. She'd have to ask Mrs. Prescott about this. Mrs. Prescott always gave her the best advice for dealing with situations. Who cared if Brendan and Carlina thought it was weird? Evvie might have been everyone's ear, their shoulder to cry on, but Evvie needed an ear, too. And that was Fiona Prescott.

Fiona was the sweetest, most motherly woman on earth. But the best thing was, she could tell her things she couldn't tell her own mother—embarrassing things, things that she was ashamed of. Fiona was the one who listened with understanding, every time Evvie felt slighted by people. Every time Carlina took center-stage. Every time she felt guys like Brendan would never notice her. Carlina never understood that. Never.

She rushed back to her room and quickly got changed into jeans and a t-shirt. Grabbing her keys, she went out to her car, smiling.

Sure, maybe Brendan had seemed a little distant this morning, but it was likely all in her head. He hadn't slipped out in the middle of the night. He'd wanted to go for another round. Like he said, he'd text her. And then maybe they could go out. Once, of course, all this drama with Carlina's murder died down.

And she'd treat him well. Unlike Carlina, she'd make him her world. He'd never look at another girl. She'd make sure of it.

She slid into the front of her old Toyota, fluffed her hair, and smiled at her reflection in the rear-view mirror. She still had the post-sex glow she'd heard so much about, a flush on her cheeks. She couldn't wait to tell Prescott that she and Brendan were finally together.

She was about to tilt the mirror back when she noticed something dark in the back seat of her car. It appeared to be . . . no, that was silly . . . it was just a trick of the eye . . .

She turned to check it out, to confirm it wasn't another person, when the black form moved. Icy tendrils of fear pricked at her neck as something snapped tight around it. The air escaped her lungs in a rush.

The shock gripped her. Someone… in her car… choking her.

Her body started to shake in fear as her hands jolted up to find the piece of cloth tight around her throat.

This wasn't happening. Carlina's killer? After her, now, too? What had she done? She was imagining this…

But the explosion of pain in her chest told her that this was no nightmare.

"Stop," she thought, but couldn't find the air to say the word. Couldn't find the energy.

And whoever was doing this clearly had no intention of stopping. Her hands pinwheeled out, finding the car horn. She laid the heel of her hand on it, emitting an ear-splitting sound.

But then, her assailant tightened the grip on her neck even more, yanking her backwards so that she could no longer reach the horn. She kicked out her legs, but that did no good. She could feel herself getting dizzy, her vision swimming as her eyes bulged. Her heart was beating so fast that it hurt and her shaking hands were loosening their grip on whatever was around her throat, something rough, tearing painfully at her skin. Tears streamed down her cheeks.

Like Marlene. Like Carlina. She was just another notch in Brendan's belt.

And like Marlene, like Carlina, she was going to die.

That was the last thought her brain was able to process before everything went dark.

CHAPTER TWENTY ONE

David Hunter had been heading over to the South Street Mall in Waco when he got the text from Mia. *Saw him at the mall. He attacked me. He's in the service hallway on the first floor, next to the lingerie shop.*

He shook his head. Sure, she was going to stay out of it.

Well, she had, for about half a day. That was probably the best record he could hope for from Mia. But now she was really being reckless. Not only was she in danger of being found by the Feds—she was putting herself in a dangerous situation with potential suspects? Not good.

He deleted the text, like all the other ones she'd sent him, as he pulled into the parking lot of the mall. There, he saw a couple of police cars, lights flashing, parked out front.

Pulling behind them, he flashed his badge. "What's going on here?"

"We got a call of what someone thought might be a domestic disturb—" The young officer stopped and studied the badge. "Whoa. What's the FBI doing here?"

He motioned inside. "Did you check out the place?"

"We were just about to."

"Come on," he said, running inside. He stopped at the map, found the location of the lingerie shop on the first floor, and rushed toward it, the police officers on his heels.

When they reached the shop, a woman greeted them by waving. "Hi. Over here."

David skidded to a stop in front of her and looked around. "You called in the disturbance."

She nodded. "I thought it was a couple fighting, so I called. But then I went over there and the guy's down. He's in that hallway. I don't see the girl. I think we need an ambulance."

David put up a hand and hurried to the hall, hand on his gun. When he reached the hallway, he saw a man, leaning up against the wall, dazed. He took out his gun. "FBI! Show me your hands."

The guy glanced at them and raised his hands.

As David came closer, he recognized the man. Sure enough, it was Peter Willington.

"Cuff him and bring him in," he told the officers.

"For what?" the guy spat, blood spraying over his bottom lip.

"Assault."

He snorted. "In case you didn't notice, I'm the one who was assaulted!" he said, rising to his feet. "I was just sitting in the mall, minding my own business before my shift. Some crazy bitch just attacked me, out of nowhere."

Mia. She was a bit crazy, a bit bitch. There was no question.

But why the hell had she done it? This was a big problem. Even worse than showing up at Evelyn Rhinehart's house and questioning her. Now, she could be in some serious trouble.

"We'll sort this out downtown."

"Hell, no. I'm not going anywhere! I know my rights!" he shouted. "And my dad is mayor of Dallas! You guys need to find that bitch. I can describe her."

Shit, David thought. *That is the last thing I want you to do.*

"Calm down," David said quietly.

"Screw you," he said, pointing at the cameras above them. "And hell yes, I want to press charges! The whole thing's on camera, so you can see for yourself. I was just minding my own damn business and she chased me."

A woman, standing behind David, said, "He's always watching my girls at the lingerie shop. He's a total stalker."

David eyed him. "You a stalker?"

He scowled at the woman. "Last thing I heard, *looking* ain't stalking. All I do, all I ever done is look."

"Right. There've been reports of you looking in girls' windows."

He shook his head. "Not me."

"And you were just looking in the girl's locker room at Oak Cliff High School, three years ago."

Peter threw up his hands. "Jesus! What's with people these days? I was a kid! I made a stupid mistake! I ain't done a thing wrong, since then. There's nothing you can pin on me. I'm clean." He wiped at his bloody nose with the back of his hand. "I can have your badges for this. Once my father finds out about this, you guys are in a world of trouble!"

David motioned to the police. “Take him in. We’ll deal with him down there.” He looked at him. “We have some questions for you about the murder of Carlina Adams.”

He rolled his eyes. “Right. I bet. I don’t know her. And so be prepared for a whole hell of a lot of I-don’t-knows. ‘Cause I’m telling you, I really don’t know a thing about her.”

“You went to school with her.”

“And? I went to school with lots of girls. I looked at ‘em. If she was hot, I probably looked more than once. But that’s all. That’s all, man. I’m telling you, you got it all wrong.”

He waved him off. “We’ll see about that.”

He motioned for the police to take him away and turned to the woman who’d called in the disturbance as the crowd began to dissipate. “This woman . . . you get a description on her?”

“She had a green sweatshirt and jeans,” she said. “That’s all I saw. Her hood was up, but from her shape I could tell she was a woman.”

Bingo. Mia. “Did you see where she went?”

She shook her head. “I think she must’ve gone out the exit because I never saw her go past the store again.”

He nodded and walked the rest of the way down the hall. Pushing open the service doors, he peered outside to the vast parking lot, now filling up with cars. Twenty minutes had passed since the assault was called in. Mia really could’ve gone anywhere, by now.

He went outside to his car, gnawing on the inside of his cheek. Something about this guy just seemed wrong. He was a pervert, yeah . . . but was he a murderer? And they’d just gotten the autopsy results on Carlina. There’d been no DNA evidence left behind at all, no sign of sexual assault. Same as with Marlene. When was the last time a pervert had murdered a couple of women . . . and there was no sign whatsoever of sexual assault?

Something was off.

As he turned his key in the ignition, his phone began to ring. He glanced at the display and groaned. Briggs.

He checked the time on his phone. Briggs was probably calling to give him shit for missing the meeting he was supposed to be in.

Reluctantly, he answered. “Hunter, here.”

“Where’ve you been, Agent?” He said with a smug lilt in his voice. “Following a big lead, huh?”

David frowned. “As a matter of fact—”

"Well, you followed the wrong one. We have another murder on our hands."

"What?" There had to be some mistake. "When?"

"Looks like it happened this morning. Body was found about an hour ago, in the driveway of her house."

"Connected?"

"Looks like it. Same MO, it looks like. Young female victim. 1531 Cypress Street."

He repeated the address back to him. Now, why did that address sound familiar? In a rush, it occurred to him. "Wait. Isn't that—"

"Evelyn Rhinehart. That's right."

"Shit. I'm on my way." He threw his phone in the passenger's seat and sped out of the parking lot. As he did, he fumbled around, trying to get his phone back. Then, with one hand, he punched in a text to Mia as he drove.

Evelyn R was just found dead at her home.

CHAPTER TWENTY TWO

Shaking, Mia pulled into a cul-de-sac a few blocks away from Evelyn Rhinehart's home.

Stepping out, she took a roundabout route there, through the wooded areas surrounding the house and the back fences of her neighbors. It took her close to the place where Carlina's body had been discovered. She crouched in the bushes, watching as the police swarmed Evvie's home and car, parked in the driveway. From where she stood, she could just make out the outline of Evvie's slim frame, slumped in the front seat.

A tear slipped down her cheek, but she swiped it away.

She could've stopped this. But instead, she'd been too wrapped up in Peter. If she hadn't told that lead to David, maybe he could've prevented it.

The best thing for everyone would be if she just went away.

She was about to when she saw David's car pull up at the crime scene. He stepped out and jogged across the street to the Rhineharts' driveway. He stooped to peer in at the dead body, then turned away, shaking his head.

Mia dragged her hands down her face, again and again, trying to understand what this meant.

It meant Peter wasn't the killer. It meant it likely wasn't a transient. It meant that whoever was doing these killings was picking these people off for a reason.

Evelyn. She was Carlina's best friend. Carlina told her all of her secrets. Did she know something? If so, what? She hadn't told Mia anything.

As Mia watched, another car pulled up, and that same woman who'd confronted Mia at the door of Evelyn's house threw open the door and ran up the driveway. It was Evelyn's mother. She sunk down on the pavement and began to bawl. A short, gray-haired man followed, wrapping his arms around her. Evelyn's father.

Yet another family, destroyed, because of this killer.

Because law enforcement had failed to keep them safe.

She buried her face in her hands.

Suddenly, her phone buzzed.

Hey.

It was from David. She looked up to see him, looking her way. He lowered his head and started to text again.

I see you. You're in danger here. Get out.

He was right. She was being reckless again. She started to back away when she saw him sending another text.

I'll meet you behind the post office around the corner in 5.

She nodded and backed off, keeping down, and headed toward her car. Checking to make sure no one was near, she got in and drove to the post office. It was a good place to meet, considering it was Sunday. A couple of trucks were parked in the back trucking bays, but there was no one around. The lot itself was surrounded by trees.

As promised, David pulled into the parking lot as she was getting out of her car.

He stopped in front of her and rolled down his window. He looked tired. "So . . . yeah. Same shit, different day."

"It was the same killer?"

"Yeah. No doubt about it. She was strangled while getting into her car, probably about an hour ago."

"In broad daylight?" she asked, shivering despite the warmth of the day. "Were there any witnesses?"

He shook his head. "One woman said she thought she heard a car horn. The neighbor who found her, the guy who lives across the street, went to get gas in his car and when he came back, he noticed the back door of the car was open and went to check it out. That's when he found her."

"Did he notice anything off as he was leaving?"

"Yeah. He saw a kid with blonde hair leaving the house, about fifteen minutes before. He thought he saw the victim in the front door of her house. Supposedly, the parents were going away for a romantic weekend upstate, so they asked him to keep an eye on the house and their daughter."

"A kid with blonde hair . . . do you think that's . . . "

"Brendan?" He shrugged. "Yeah. Her phone was in her cup holder. It wasn't locked. She'd been texting him, the night before. Forensics is in there right now, collecting evidence. From what I can see, she definitely had a male guest over last night. If he's the killer, he's not all that bright—he left a lot of evidence all over her bed, if you know what I mean."

She hugged herself tighter, warding off another chill. "That's taking a lot of chances."

"Speaking of taking chances . . ." He eyed her.

"I know, I know. That was stupid, with Peter."

He gave her a look that said, *You think?* "Yeah. And you coming here? That's stupid, too. You need to stay away."

She sighed. "I will. I want to. But look at that. The killer taking chances like that? It means he's desperate. He's going to be easier to catch right now."

"Yeah. And I'll do the catching. You need to get out of here."

"Okay, but what are you going to do? We don't have any leads."

"We have a couple ideas."

"Like?"

"Like . . . I'm going to head over and interview Brendan again. And then I was going to check out this Frederick kid. Her boyfriend. There might've been a jealousy element to it."

"That makes sense. You interview him before?"

"Yeah. But he was kind of a dud. A little dim-witted. But who knows?"

"Anything else from her phone?"

"Yeah. From her texts, we know where she was headed. To a place called Rafferty's, downtown. It looks like she was meeting with a Fiona Prescott. She's a guidance counselor at the high school."

"But she graduated last year. Why would—"

"I know. She and Evelyn met up a lot. I guess they remained friends after graduation."

"How about the school? Have you been there?"

He nodded. "I've been there. Briggs and his men have been there. We've asked around. There's not much of anything there. Why?"

She shrugged. "Well, Marlene and Carlina were on the same soccer team, and they were both the pretty, popular, outgoing types. But Evelyn, from everything I see, was a bit more awkward and shy and kept to herself. She was Carlina's best friend, but other than that, a totally different kind of girl. So there's only a couple things tying all three girls together."

"Brendan."

"Yeah. And, the high school."

David nodded. "Right. You think I should take another look?"

"No. I mean, if you've already checked it out, I suppose there's no reason. You probably won't find anything else."

But I might, she thought, gnawing on her lip. *Fresh eyes always help.*

"Right," he said, eyeing her suspiciously. "So . . . where are you heading to, next?"

She reached for her car door. "I should probably leave town. But text me if you hear anything, okay?"

"Will do. Take care," he said, stepping on the gas, leaving her alone in the parking lot.

She stood in his dust, watching him leave, and let out a big breath. *I should probably do just what I promised and leave town,* she thought to herself. *But the problem is, I don't think I can. Not until I have my man.*

*

Oak Cliff High School was a sprawling, modern building on a hill, one of the newest high schools in Dallas. It had a gleaming white façade and a sign outside with the words OAK CLIFF SENIOR HIGH SCHOOL, with an electronic bulletin board underneath that read, *FLY HIGH ANGEL CARLINA! RIP.*

Normally, the place was probably crawling with people, and the lot full of cars and buses. But now, there were only a couple cars, parked near the very front of one of the entrances. It was Sunday afternoon, after all.

She pulled close to the few cars and stepped out, then went to the door. It was locked, of course.

Using her hands as a shield to block out the light, she leaned into the door, trying to see inside.

An old janitor was wheeling a cart with a garbage can, down the hallway. She waved at him, and he held up a finger and came over. When he opened the door, he said, "What can I do you for, Miss?"

"Hi. I'm . . . a new parent. I just moved to the area," she said, surprising herself with how easily the lie came out. "My daughter would be a freshman here, but I was thinking of one of the private schools in the area."

"Ah," he said, shaking his head. "My kids all go here. This place is great. Brand new. State of the art everything. You couldn't want a better place to send your kids."

"Really?" She scanned past him. "Because the private school I was looking at—"

He pushed aside the door. "You come on in and I'll give you the grand tour. I promise, you won't want to send your kid anywhere else."

"Oh! Would you? Thanks! That would be super," she said, stepping inside.

"Yeah, I'm not supposed to have guests here, but I been here since the school opened four years ago and they ain't given me a raise, yet. They should! I'm the best advertising this place gets. Ha."

He led her to a bright foyer with a stained-glass ceiling. Above her, bathed in light, was the school's insignia and mascot. *FLY HIGH SILVER EAGLES!* It read. The foyer was also adorned with many glass cases, filled with various awards.

"This is impressive," she said, turning slowly. "Looks very nice."

"Gets even better," he said, walking her down the long hallway to a set of double doors. "Look at this."

He pushed open a door to a massive gymnasium. "Wow," she said, her voice echoing.

"You go down that hallway to get to the pool. Olympic sized."

Mia raised her eyebrows. "That's great. But you know, after the news I've read . . ."

"Ah," he said, shaking his head. "I got you. You mean those girls that were murdered."

"Right. Did you know the girls, Mr. . . .?"

"Davidson. No. I didn't. But it's a shame."

Something prickled the back of her neck. Davidson. D. She wondered if David had looked into this guy. "Do you have any idea what happened? You think it could've been a classmate or something?"

He shrugged. "Nah. People around here, at this school, sure are nice. That's what I said, when I got here. Everyone's so *nice*. My kids said so, too."

"Did they know the girls?"

"Yeah. My oldest. She played soccer with the girls. Didn't really care for them. Said they were a little stuck up. A little wild, too. Kind of boy-crazy, if you know what I mean, talking about sex and drugs and things my girl ain't into," he said with a shrug. "They moved pretty fast. I figure it was probably one of the boys they got themselves tied up with."

"Someone who went to the school?"

He shook his head. "Nah. There was that one kid, the football player. Always hanging around them. But they had secrets. And they forget," he held up a huge ring of keys, attached with a cord to his belt, "I've got the key to their lockers."

Mia stared at them, agog. "Did you go through their lockers?"

A sly little grin touched his face. "Sure did." He looked around carefully. "It's my job to clean out their lockers. And maybe I wasn't supposed to pry, but the girl was dead, and I was curious. And you know what I seen in Marlene's locker?"

She leaned forward, interested. "What?"

"There was a little something written on that girl, Marlene's, Physics notebook. In the margin. It said, *Don't tell a soul.*" He smiled. "So I think those girls were big on secrets."

That was rather vague. "What kind of secrets, though?"

"I don't know. I tried telling the police but they weren't interested. They seemed like they wanted to blame it on some guy who was just passing through, so I let it drop." He shrugged, "But I don't believe that. Whatever it was, I think it was something maybe someone would kill for. So what could that be? Had to be something pretty big."

But what? Mia gnashed her teeth. "Well . . . it's a little concerning. I don't know if I want my child going someplace like that. Sounds dangerous."

"Yeah. I hear you. But most of the people at the school ain't like that. They're real nice."

He took her down the hallway to the science lab, and around to the auditorium. The layout of the school was a giant square. She oohed and aahed at the appropriate places, and then they wound up in the foyer they'd started at.

He paused in front of the restrooms and said, "Well, that's all she wrote. You should bring your kid in, for a tour, when they're open. You know. Get acquainted."

"Yeah. Maybe I will." She pointed at the restroom. "Mind if I use the facilities?"

"Oh. No. Be my guest."

"Thanks for the tour. I'm sure you're busy. I'll see myself out," she said with a smile, heading into the pink-tiled bathroom.

When she stepped in, though, she paused at the door. She listened as the sound of his squeaky-wheeled garbage can grew fainter and fainter as he continued down the hall. When she could no longer hear it, she slipped outside and stole across the foyer, to the main office.

The door was already open. She crept through, around a counter, and to the nearest computer. There, she jiggled the mouse. The computer came alive, showing the OCHS computer system. She clicked on the Student Schedule button, constantly looking up through the glass wall to make sure the janitor wasn't coming back.

When she got to a search bar, she typed in: *Carlina Adams,* and entered the previous year.

Carlina Adams's schedule popped up. The girl was taking a lot of heavy, Honors-level classes—AP Physics, AP Computer Science, AP Literature, AP Calculus.

Definitely pushing herself, Mia thought. *But I guess that's what one has to do, to get into Tulane.*

She then typed in Marlene Dotts. That brought up a different schedule, but no less challenging. There were a lot of AP classes, including AP Physics—period six.

Mia went back to Carlina's schedule. Sure enough, AP Physics, period six.

Maybe Marlene had written that note, *Don't tell a soul,* to Carlina, in Physics class?

She wished she could have some confirmation. Something. Were they lab partners? If she could've gotten into her locker to see, maybe she'd have more information. But all that evidence was probably locked up tight, in some basement at the police station.

Out of curiosity, she clicked on the course, and it brought up the name of the teacher.

Kirk Donovan.

D.

Don't tell a soul.

Did something begin there, last year, that they didn't want anyone to know about? Something involving this Kirk Donovan? Is that what had started all of this?

She wasn't sure. But it was the closest she'd been in a long time.

As she stared at the name, she heard a slight squeaking out in the hall. She stiffened as she realized what it was.

The janitor was returning.

Keeping her head down, she made for the doorway of the office, then, checking to make sure he wasn't in sight, broke for the door. She pushed it open as quietly as possible and slid out, shoving it closed. It was only when she made it back to her car and had started the engine that she finally exhaled the breath she'd been holding.

She had to look into this Kirk Donovan.

CHAPTER TWENTY THREE

U.S. Marshal Kane Wilcox scrubbed a hand down his face and muttered a curse, his twelfth of the hour.

It was mid-afternoon, now. He'd been at Mia North's house, staking it out since he'd left the park, and what did he have to show for it?

Nothing.

She hadn't been at the park, either. And now, North's husband knew he was on her tail. He'd had to hang back on the street, even farther now, to stay out of Aiden North's view, which meant he could be missing something, but he didn't think so. It was too quiet.

Maybe her husband had gotten in touch with her somehow, told her to stay away. She was wise to him, now. So while he was still sure she was the type of woman who would go back to her old friends and family . . . he had a feeling this approach was no longer going to work.

He had to think of something else.

Luckily, though, he had his ideas.

He reached over and grabbed the Big Gulp from the cup holder and sucked down a little more of his now-watery blue raspberry Slurpee. Then he pushed open the ever-thickening folder that had been occupying a prominent spot on the front passenger seat of his car.

He paged through pictures of Mia, a graduation photo from the FBI Academy, photos of her with her daughter and husband, photos of her sister Francine and of her parents, both Dallas Police officers. He'd been keeping tabs on all of them, only to find absolutely nothing. If she'd been in contact with him, it hadn't been in person.

But he didn't think she'd risk contacting them via phone, either, since that could destroy their livelihoods. Or would she? If she was staying in touch, it was probably with just one person, so she could limit the damage. But who?

When he flipped to another photograph, he had his answer.

David L. Hunter, thirty-five. FBI Agent for nearly three and a half years, and Mia North's junior partner. He was African-American, good-looking, body-builder, former military, too. Went into the U.S.

Army right out of high school, with a long line of decoration from two tours in Afghanistan. After the military, he graduated with honors from UT Austin in only two years, got his law degree from Rice in two, also. Married young, before he went into the military, one son, Louis Hunter, aged nine. Recently divorced.

Looking at that, one would think that David Hunter was the type of man who played by the rules.

But looking deeper, Kane saw the cracks in the façade. The man was newly divorced, with a young kid. He probably understood what it was like for a family to fall apart. He'd be sympathetic to Mia.

He paged through some more. He'd provided some interesting testimony that had convicted Mia North of the crime of murder. Afterwards, though, he'd said to a reporter that he felt she was innocent and wrongfully convicted, and that he didn't "think she was capable of murder in cold blood."

To Kane Wilcox, that smacked of one thing: Guilt.

Like him, David Hunter had a strong sense of justice, of wanting to set things right. And if they were wrong, and if, more importantly, he was the one who'd made them that way?

He'd do everything in his power to atone for his mistakes.

Yes. David Hunter was his man.

He punched his home address into his GPS, started his car and headed out to pay him a visit. As he was driving, though, he thought better of it. It was early in the afternoon, and an agent like Hunter wouldn't be home. He punched in a call to his old Operation Desert Storm buddy from the Dallas Field Office, Special Agent in Charge Matthew Pembroke.

"Pembroke, here."

"Long time, no talk, buddy. It's Wilcox."

"Wilcox! How's life treating you?"

"Good, good. Hey. I'm in town and I need your help. Can you give me details on an agent of yours, David Hunter?"

"Shit," he muttered. "Don't tell me. Is this about—"

"Yeah. I can't say more. Just tell me where he is."

A pause. "He's in Oak Cliff. Investigating a murder of a couple of teens. He just called in from the scene of a third one. He was heading to the police precinct there."

"Got it. Thanks. Let's catch up soon while I'm in town. Later."

He ended the call and punched the new information into his GPS, then navigated to the station. The area of Oak Cliff in Dallas was a pretty little place, nice for families, with kids playing frisbee in the park and families walking their dogs on the sidewalks. There'd been three teenagers murdered here? Hell.

*

Inside the one-story brick building, he flashed his badge to the young officer, who visibly blanched. "Looking for FBI agent David Hunter," he said, scanning the area as he slipped the credentials into his pocket and fixed his suit jacket. "Is he here?"

The kid gulped. "Yeah. Um—one second."

He tripped on the chair legs as he stood up and ran to talk to a supervising officer. Kane continued to survey the WANTED and MISSING posters on the wall, aware that the two men were just behind him, discussing his presence.

A moment later, a big man with a ruddy face and a scrub-brush of red hair approached, a warning look on his face. "Agent Wilcox? I'm Lieutenant Briggs. Come this way."

He led him behind the waiting area, and down a hallway, into a conference room that was spread out with various laptops and photographs and items belonging to an investigation. A couple of officers in uniform were there, in addition to a man in dress pants and a white shirt, sleeves rolled up, whose total attention was focused on a laptop screen.

He pointed at something and was just about to say something to one of the officers when Briggs said, with a smug tinge to his voice, "Hey, Hunter. You've got a friend, here."

Hunter's face fell to a frown. "Who are you?"

"Kane Wilcox. U.S. Marshal."

Hunter's jaw set. He didn't speak, but from the look on his face, Kane knew that if he did, it'd be one word: *Shit.*

"Can I speak to you in private, please?" He glanced around at the officers.

Briggs motioned to them. "Come on, boys."

The officers left, and Kane closed the door behind them. "I think you might have an idea of why I'm here?"

Hunter ran an eye over the conference table. "No. Actually. No clue."

He opened the button on his suit jacket and thrust his hands into his pockets. "Your partner Mia North, a convicted criminal, has been a wanted fugitive for the better part of a month and you have no idea why I'm here?"

He shrugged, but didn't meet his eye. "She hasn't been my partner for some time. I've been getting on without her, Agent."

"Have you?"

He motioned to the files on the table. "As you can see, this case really needs my attention."

"Yes, so I hear. What's the deal with this?"

"These girls were murdered. Two in the last few days."

He approached the table and looked over the photographs of the pretty girls. Mia North had been big into solving cases involving young people. "This would've been right up your partner's alley, huh?"

Hunter let out a breath. "Murder of a kid? No. She liked the missing persons cases. The ones where there was still hope the kid could be found alive."

"Sounds like you had a lot of respect for her."

He bristled, and for the first time, met Kane's eye. "Why don't you just cut the bullshit and ask what you're really insinuating here? Am I helping Mia North? The answer is no."

Kane crossed his arms over his chest. "When was the last time you were in touch with her?"

"She's tried to be in touch with me over the past month. Sending me notes, things like that. I've ignored them."

"You didn't report them?"

He shook his head. "I was part of the prosecution's case and a big reason why she was put away. After that, I decided I'd done enough."

Kane nodded. "May I see these notes she sent you?"

"I threw them away."

"She hasn't tried to phone or text you?"

He dug into his pocket and lifted his phone. "Want to have a look?"

Was he bluffing? If he was, he was good at it. Kane shook his head. "So the last time you heard from her . . ."

"I don't know. A week ago. Maybe two." He glanced back at the table.

"You sound upset, Agent."

He snorted. "Yeah. Three girls are dead. I'm trying to do my job. And right now, you're standing in the way of it. So pardon me if I don't offer to make you a cup of tea so we can sit down and have a nice long chat about my former partner. I can't concern myself with her poor decisions. I have other things on my mind right now."

Kane stared at him, his suspicions aroused. He'd gone from protective, not wanting to get her in trouble by reporting her contact to his supervisor—to unconcerned and completely devoid of compassion for her, in practically one breath. There was definitely something to this that David Hunter wasn't saying.

"Thank you, Agent," he said, turning on his heel.

When he stepped outside, he found Lieutenant Briggs standing at the door. Had he been listening? Kane nodded at him. "Thank you for your t--"

"I wouldn't believe him, if I were you."

That piqued his interest. "Hmm?"

"You're looking for Mia, right?"

He crossed his arms and leaned a shoulder against the wall. "Perhaps. What do you know of her?"

"I knew her dad. Worked with him on a few cases before he retired. I worked with her a few times. It didn't surprise any of us when she was arrested for that murder. She took a lot of those cases way too personal, 'cause of her family history. You know. Sam Jr."

He nodded. "Her brother who was kidnapped and murdered by an unknown assailant."

"That's right. There's been a screw loose in all them Clopeckis—that's Mia's maiden name—since then. I'm amazed she even made it into the Feds, knowing all the psych tests you guys are exposed to."

He let out a grunt. Most agents, though, had their own skeletons. He certainly had his. "What did you mean about Hunter?"

Briggs shrugged. "He's just been pretty shifty lately. Heading off on leads, and we have no idea how he got them. Made us think he had a silent partner, if you know what I mean."

That was interesting. "Have any of your men heard or seen anything from Mia North?"

"Oh, yeah. In fact, we got a call the other day from a mother who said a woman fitting her description was going around, interviewing possible suspects." He shrugged. "Then again, could've just been a reporter."

"Did you look into it?"

"As much as we could. There are always rumors. Sightings. Every day. So many, you don't know what's fact and what's fiction, and we can't look into them all. A lot of the guys think of her as some sort of legend, but I think she's dumb as shit. If she was smart, she'd have flown off to Mexico by now. But I don't know. Maybe she's hanging around, thinking she can prove her innocence. Who knows? That's a long shot."

He handed the lieutenant a business card with his information. "If you think of anything that can help. Again. Thanks. I'll be in touch if I have any more questions."

"Of course. Anything else we can do for you, Agent, you just let us know!"

He stepped outside into the dying light of day, thinking of what Agent David Hunter had said. He didn't trust he was telling the truth.

And that meant that he'd stick around and keep digging. Eventually, the truth always came out.

CHAPTER TWENTY FOUR

Mia pulled onto a wooded side-street near the high school and placed the call, her mind whirling with all the things she'd learned so far.

"Yeah?"

"David?" she asked, surprised by his gruff tone of voice. "Is everything all right?"

He let out a long sigh. "I just left the police station after having a conversation with a U.S. Marshal Kane Wilcox."

She stiffened. "Oh."

"Yeah, *oh*." He paused. "I sure as hell hope you're hiding yourself somewhere good, because he is right on your tail. If he'd decided to confiscate my phone . . . it'd be all over. For both of us."

"I know. I—"

"You're hiding, right? I get the feeling I already know the answer to that question. You wouldn't be calling me if you were. Geez, girl. You're in deep shit, and dragging me down with you."

"Yeah, but listen to me," she said excitedly. "I compared Carlina and Marlene's schedules. And they both share a Physics class. And Marlene wrote a—"

"Compared their schedules?" he spoke over her. "And how did you do that, I wonder? Let me guess. You—"

"Yes. I went to the high school. But—"

"Jesus! Mia!"

"Listen to me! Just listen—"

"No. I'm done listening to you, Mia. The more you dig, the more you find. The more you find, the more you keep digging. And don't you get it? You're digging a grave for the both of us! And I can't have it anymore."

The desperation in his voice was heartbreaking. It stunned her speechless.

"Look. I got to look out for myself. For my Louis. I can't do this anymore," he said quietly. "So I want you to stay out of this investigation. For good. Let me handle it. And don't contact me again, you hear me?"

He didn't wait for an answer. The line went dead.

She sat there with the phone against her ear, hand trembling.

He was right. He was risking so much to be in contact with her, and he had just as much to lose. If he continued, he'd most certainly lose his job, and he could be put away in prison for a long time. He'd lose his family, too. He'd lose everything she'd already lost.

She couldn't do that to him.

But she couldn't contact her family, either, or put them in danger. This U.S. Marshal was closing in, making it more and more dangerous, with every passing day.

So she was alone. Completely alone.

And if she wanted to stop bringing pain to the people she cared about, she'd have to stay that way.

But what could she do, alone?

Nothing.

She couldn't think of a single thing. Oh, she could poke into different places like the high school, but anytime she met anyone, it was only increasing her chances of being found by the Marshals. She wasn't an island. She needed the help of people to get through. David, her family, people like Nita Franklin . . . they were the reason she'd made it this far.

With that thought in her mind, she started the car and drove aimlessly, away from the city.

*

Two hours later, when she arrived in Waco, she stopped to get gas. As she was filling up, she looked around at the unfamiliar sights of the town. If she kept driving down Interstate 35, she could be at the Mexican border by midnight. There was a good chance that the Marshals had put out a bulletin, warning the Border Patrol Agents that she might try to cross there, so it might be safer to try to enter at McAllen. Then, she could live in Mexico. Maybe even try to travel East to the gulf cities. Maybe even go as far as Playa del Carmen. She'd vacationed there once. She could live the rest of her life, on a beach, without a care in the world.

But of course, it was always the thought of Kelsey and Aiden that pulled her back.

Such a thought was impossible. It would be like tearing out her own heart.

Once she filled her gas tank, she got herself a soda and chips and pulled into a space in an empty office park.

She watched as the sun slowly sank below the horizon, dappling its orange and pink rays across the cloud-dotted sky. The effect over the desert was breathtaking, something she appreciated all the more, knowing how close she'd come to never being able to see sights like this, again.

If U.S. Marshal Kane Wilcox had his way, this might be her last.

But she needed to stop feeling sorry for herself. People had it worse. People like Marlene, Carlina, Evvie—cut down in their prime, just when they were beginning to live.

They needed justice.

And though she might have been a fugitive, she wasn't completely down and out.

In fact, she might have had an advantage. David would have to go through the proper channels to make things happen. She didn't have to, anymore. She could go places the cops couldn't. Be unruly. Shake things up. Take chances that could bring this murderer out into the open.

She looked down at the paper she'd stuffed into the cupholder when she'd gotten out of the high school. It said, simply, two words. KIRK DONOVAN.

David didn't know about him. No one did.

It was her lead to pursue, if she just had the courage.

She pulled out of the parking space, and pointed her car north. She had to find this Physics teacher and see what he had to say for himself.

CHAPTER TWENTY FIVE

Mia stared at her phone and punched the steering wheel.

There were twenty-four listings for Kirk Donovans online.

She typed in *Kirk Donovan Physics OCHS,* and while that provided a listing on the high school website, it didn't include a home address.

And she sure wasn't going to go around to all of them, trying to find the right one. If she did that, that was a sure ticket to getting herself picked up by the Marshals.

She clicked on the bio for Kirk Donovan at OCHS.

Mr. Kirkman graduated maxima cum laude with a B.A. in Physics and a B.A. in Mathematics from Rice University and went on to earn an M.A. and Ph.D. in Physics from Princeton University. He joins the faculty of OCHS teaching Physics, which he had regarded as his calling in life. His dissertation, "Transient optomechanical phenomena related to optomechanical light storage," received the top honor from the American Science Teachers Association. Other areas of Mr. Donovan's interests include LEGO, Quantum Mechanics theory and effects, Philosophy of Science and scientific toys & demonstrations. He lives in Dallas where he is an active member of the Association of Physical Sciences and the Society of Physics Students at UT Dallas.

Mia blinked as she read it all. *Wow. What a nerd.*

Then she scrolled down to the photograph of the man.

Probably in his mid-forties, he was fully bald up top, with patches of scraggly brown hair around his ears. His glasses were thick and round, Harry Potter-like. His face was wide and flat. The tip of his nose pointed downward, and his eyes, though magnified by the thick lenses, were still rather beady, giving him the overall look of a serpent. He was wearing a bow-tie, slightly askew, and his smile bore crooked teeth.

In other words, not very attractive.

Immediately, Mia's suspicions took a turn.

For the past hour, she'd been weaving a story that explained the motive for the murders. Mia had been imagining Marlene in a torrid affair with a handsome young teacher. Stranger things had happened. And perhaps, she'd threatened to tell. And so he'd had her murdered.

Then, perhaps, Carlina had started an affair with him and threatened to tell the authorities. And so he'd had her murdered, too. And Evvie? Well, Carlina and Evvie were best friends. Maybe he'd thought she needed to be silenced, too.

But this man? He hardly looked like the kind of guy who'd engage in a secret relationship, who beautiful girls would be throwing themselves at.

She sighed. Maybe she was barking up another wrong tree.

Of course, if she could just take a look at those journals, she would know for sure.

David had said the police had looked, but Mia knew what kind of "looking" they usually did, especially when the FBI took over the investigation and told them to. It was probably very cursory. So it hadn't surprised her that they only found one journal. That was probably the journal she hadn't hidden very well, because it was the least incriminating. The others . . .

Maybe they simply required a little more digging the police had not been willing to do.

She shifted her car into drive and headed to the Adams residence.

*

As predicted, the Adams residence was dark. Carlina's parents were still away. The house itself seemed eerily silent. She drove past carefully, watching to see if anyone was keeping an eye on the home. But there was no one.

Parking in the same place she'd parked earlier, she stole through the woods and into the back of the house. The door was once again locked, but she easily picked it, again, and climbed up the stairs to Carlina's room.

More things had been removed from the room. Whoever had gone through it this latest time had left a bit of a mess—mattress and furniture overturned, the contents of her dresser spilled. Mia hovered in the doorway, thinking.

If I was going to hide a journal under a floorboard where no one would look, where would I do it?

At first, she turned to the closet. But as she took a step toward it, she hesitated.

Actually, that would be the first place anyone would look. She could just bet that the police had found that single journal in there.

She turned on her phone flashlight and aimed its beam inside the open accordion doors of the closet. Sure enough, a floorboard had been removed.

Spinning, she looked at the vanity, the dresser, the bed.

Bed? No, that was another sure bet. If she *really* wanted to hide it . . .

She wouldn't hide it under a floorboard at all.

Mia's eyes instinctively went upward, then, to the vent above Carlina's silk tufted headboard.

Worth a shot.

She pulled the mattress back onto the frame and stepped on it, then climbed onto the night table. From there, she pointed the flashlight into the dusty register.

Sure enough, she could see the rumpled pages of a book.

Her heart sped in her chest as she looked around for something to turn the screws on the vent cover. But then she realized that she didn't need to. They were loose, as if Carlina had turned them many times before to hide her private thoughts away from the world.

Mia smiled as she pulled the cover away from the wall. There was a stack of dusty books there.

She pulled one down. The worn pleather cover said, in gold foil, *Memories.*

Mia opened to the first page and read:

I hate her.

People think we are friends, but that's by design. Keep your friends close and your enemies closer. And that's what I do.

Everything Marlene wants, she gets. The Striker on our soccer team. Class treasurer. NHS president. She even got accepted to Stanford, Early Decision. She's Miss Perfect. Miss Do-No-Wrong.

Everything I want, I lose to her. That's just the way of it.

I used to be okay with it. I used to just grin and bear it.

But not this year. It's my senior year, and I'm determined to shake things up. So I will. I'm going to take what's mine. Starting with her boyfriend. And then I'm going to make sure she can never show her face in this town again.

Just watch.

- *C*

Mia looked up. That was interesting. So they weren't even friends. They were outright enemies?

She flipped forward a few pages.

Oh, it is going sooooo good!

Christmas went by with a bunch of fireworks. Everyone is putty in my hands, really. All I had to do was leave a few carefully-placed notes in D's mailbox, and he bought it, hook, line, and sinker. He thought Marlene had a crush on him. And, well . . . he's a guy, and he's desperate. He took advantage of that information in only the way he could.

I've been talking to her more and more after practice and now she thinks she can confide in me. She thinks we're best buddies. So she told me that he asked her to his house to "Study." I asked what she was going to do. Really, I thought she'd just be worried about keeping her grades so he wouldn't jeopardize her chances at Stanford, but what she said blew me away! She's actually into him. She told me she wants to be with him—like really be with him! That dork! But she thinks he's hot. I don't know what she sees in him . . .

I guess it's the whole "hot for teacher," forbidden romance thing.

Anyway . . . I casually mentioned to Brendan that I thought they'd broken up because I saw Marlene with someone else . . . now the trap is set.

This is always my favorite time . . . right before the fireworks.

- C

Hot for teacher. D. Donovan. Marlene actually had a relationship with Kirk Donovan, and Carlina orchestrated it? Mia's pulse pounded, and she quickly flipped to the next entry, a week later.

Oh, my God.

Listening to Marlene detail her night with Donovan . . . at first, I wanted to throw up in my mouth a little. Because it's Dorky Donovan! But then, it actually sounded really sweet. A real adult. And he told her he couldn't wait for her to graduate so they could be together, for real.

Blech.

Anyway, Operation Steal Boyfriend is almost complete. Brendan's coming over tonight, to "talk." He's playing the poor, jilted boyfriend—keeps asking me who the other guy is, but I always tell him I don't know. But tonight, I don't think there will be much talking!

Evvie tells me I should lay off him. I think she has a crush on him. As if that will ever happen. Ha ha.

- *C*

Mia quickly flipped a few more pages and her eye caught on something outlined in bright red: *OMG.*

Marlene is dead.

I can't believe this. I just got the news and my hands are shaking. She was strangled walking home from soccer practice.

Everyone's saying that Coach Loos is responsible. He was the last person we all saw talking to her, and she was yelling at him. So it makes sense.

It's possible.

But then I think about Donovan. I wonder if I should tell him what I know. He doesn't seem like the killing type . . . but does anyone?

- *C*

There was a long space between that entry and the next one. The next one was almost six months later, in August.

Wow.

Okay, so I thought I should lay off the journal for a while, just in case. But something so big has happened, I can't even think straight unless I write it down.

They didn't find Marlene's killer.

The annoying things was that Marlene became this saint. It was so annoying. People were kissing her butt so much more in death—and I didn't think that was possible! Marlene this, Marlene that, what a lovely girl, bleh!. And Donovan was interviewed and actually said she was one of the most extraordinary students he'd ever known. Vomit!

I got into Tulane, and I'll be leaving for Louisiana tomorrow. But I was bored all summer, hearing all those vomitous stories about Marlene, and wanted those fireworks again.

And boy . . . did I get them!

I went to Donovan's place in Elm Glen, just under the guise that I was going around, thanking all my teachers for such a stellar education that really prepared me to take on the world, blah blah blah. He invited me in for lemonade and cookies. While I was sitting there, in his kitchen, I let the bombshell drop.

Oh, diary, if you could see his face! He went bright purple and dropped an entire glass of lemonade on his pants.

It was so funny. So he asked me what I wanted, and I told him that if he wanted me to shut up, he needed to play by my rules.

Of course he agreed! And let me tell you . . . Marlene was right. That man is gifted in bed. He blows all the other boys I've been with, right out of the water! Now, I don't think he's thinking of Marlene. He's thinking of me.

As it should be. Mark my words. If I have my way, by next spring, I'll have her name erased from this town's memory forever.

- C

Mia flipped the page and found herself on the last entry in the book.

I'm home.

I got a text from Donovan, wanting to see me. I've been thinking about this meeting for eight months, and I know it's crazy, but I really do think I'm in love with him. After dealing with all these stupid high school and college boys, it's nice to know a real man. One who can take care of me. I can't wait.

It's going to be amazing.

I'm too excited. Evvie's all about sharing, and this time, I'm doing nothing wrong. I need to manifest this, by speaking it into the world. Besides, Kirk and I are both adults now. I'm not his student anymore. We can be together. The world just has to get used to it.

So I bit the bullet this morning. I told

Mia stared at it, her heart thumping.

She flipped the page. Squinted to see if anything had been smudged away. Nothing.

Who did she have to tell? It just seemed to end, abruptly, mid-sentence.

Carlina was a little sadistic meddler. She was the one who'd orchestrated a lot of this. And Kirk Donovan, Physics teacher, had been bearing the brunt of their secrets.

She closed the book and opened her phone, then typed in, *Kirk Donovan, Elm Glen.*

That time, an address came up.

She didn't have to guess who Carlina had told. She'd told Evvie. And the three people who knew about Marlene's secret, forbidden relationship with a teacher were now dead.

She broke for the door, reaching for her car keys.

She knew who the killer was.

She had to find Kirk Donovan.

CHAPTER TWENTY SIX

It was just before nine when Mia pulled up to the small ranch home, about five minutes down the street from Evvie and Carlina's development. Mia barely looked at the home, registering the small American flag flapping from a pole near the door and the mailbox that said, Donavon in peeling paint. She was still reeling from the words she'd read in the diary, trying to make sense of them.

She couldn't be coy or beat around the bush. She needed answers, as fast as she could get them.

She jogged up to the front door and knocked, then stepped behind a potted bush on the stoop.

Inside, a high, wobbly male voice said, "One moment."

She heard the door open, saw the light spread over the doorstep. The man there paused, then took a step out, looking both ways. He was even less impressive in person, almost her height and build, with less hair than in the photograph. He was wearing a white button-down dress shirt, like in the photo, no bow-tie, sleeves rolled up, and his hands were wet, from washing.

"Hello?" he asked, his eyes finally crossing her hiding place.

She sprang out of her spot and shoved him back, into his front foyer. He stumbled over the step and skidded onto his backside. She stepped in over his prone body, slammed the door behind him, and knelt over him, grabbing his shirt.

"Who are you?" His voice shook in fear. "What is the meaning of—"

"Listen to me, prick," she said, yanking the collar of his shirt and bringing his face even with hers as she crouched over him, straddling his narrow chest. "I already know the answer to this question but I need you to confirm it. If you try to lie to me, you know Physics, right? Your head, that wall. I'll use just enough force to make sure you're nothing but a stain on it."

His eyes widened. "W-what's the question?"

"Did you or did you not have an inappropriate relationship with one of your students? Marlene Dotts?"

"No—no. I've never had any relationship with anyone in school. Yeah, I was dating Fiona Prescott, off and on, but—"

She clutched his collar tighter. "Don't give me that. I have evidence. I've read her journals, and she names you."

His eyes broke from hers. He swallowed, and mumbled, "All right. Fine. Yes. I didn't mean to. But it just happened."

She waited for more, and in that space, she heard something sizzling in one of the rooms beyond, the sound of the kitchen fan whirring. The adrenaline drained from her muscles, and the next time she spoke, she was calmer. "And Carlina Adams?"

He swallowed with effort again. "Y-yes. But she wasn't my student at the time. She was—"

"Doesn't matter. You engaged in illegal behavior Kirk. And you killed them both to stop them from telling. Am I right?"

He shook his head fervently. "No. No, that's not right. I didn't kill anyone. I admit, I slept with those girls. But I wouldn't kill them. I—I was in love with Marlene. And Carlina . . . that was a mistake. She came to me and told me she knew about me and Marlene, told me she wouldn't tell, as long as I . . ." He squeezed his eyes closed. "Carlina always had an obsession with being just like Marlene. I always thought so. I should've known she'd do that. I don't know why Marlene told her . . ."

Mia loosened her grip on his shirt and leaned back. "And Evelyn? Did you have a relationship with her, too?"

"I didn't even know her. I swear. And if she knew anything about it, I don't know. I didn't even talk to her." He let out a long wail. "Please, please don't kill me."

"Kill you?" she murmured, confused. Did he really think she was the killer? "I'm not going to kill you."

He held up his hands. "Then what are you going to do to me?"

She let go of his shirt and sat back, shaking her head, dazed. As she did, the teacher began to sob loudly, tears pouring down his cheeks. He rolled into fetal position and began to babble. "I love Physics. I'm going to lose my job. Aren't I? Aren't I?"

She stared at him. Carlina had said in her journal, *He doesn't seem like the killing type.* That was an understatement. This mild-mannered teacher looked like he couldn't hurt a fly.

Then she sniffed. Something was burning. "Whatever you're making, you should probably turn it off." She pointed to the kitchen. "Dinner?"

He continued to sob. As she was standing up, she heard a call pulling into the driveway.

Her blood ran cold.

She jumped to her feet and peered out the side window.

Sure enough, a few cops were arriving, along with U.S. Marshal Kane Wilcox. One of them was holding Carlina's incriminating journal. *Oh, no.*

Looking around for escape and finding none, she dove for a nearby powder room, just as there was a knock on the door. "Kirk Donovan. Open up."

The cops didn't wait. They shoved open the door and advanced on Donovan, who'd only been able to rise up on his elbows.

"Kirk Donovan?" the officer said. "You're under arrest for the murders of Marlene Dotts, Carlina Adams, and Evelyn Rhinehart."

He held up his hands to shield himself, and skirted away, sobbing. "No! No! It isn't me!"

Mia pressed herself up against the wall and listened as they snapped cuffs on him. Meanwhile, his sobbing never stopped, even as they yanked him out the door. Smoke began to fill the house, and the sizzling became more violent. After a moment of listening to it, she crept toward the partially open bathroom door and peered out the crack.

Though the officers and suspects were gone, Kane Wilcox stood there in the smoky haze, scanning the foyer and frowning, as if he was a dog trying to catch the scent of something in the air.

Her heart stopped. She didn't dare move. If he turned one inch toward her, he could see her, in the darkness of the small powder room.

Then he moved forward. A moment later, the sizzling stopped. Then he left, turning off the lights behind him.

Mia exhaled and slumped against the sink in relief. Too close.

They had a man in custody, though, now. So it should've been her cue to run as fast and far away as she could. But something niggled at the back of her mind.

Is that mild-mannered Physics teacher really a cold-blooded killer?

CHAPTER TWENTY SEVEN

Mia's hands shook on the steering wheel as she drove into the night.

That was way too close. If that Marshal had pushed open the door . . .

She placed a hand on her chest to stop her heart from beating so madly.

They'd arrested a suspect. She should've been happy. The criminal had been caught.

But the more she thought about it, the more uncertain she became. He was so willing to admit to having an inappropriate relationship, and yet he adamantly refused that he'd committed the murders. And he was so weak, so sensitive. Definitely not the murdering type.

As she drove, she desperately wished she could contact David. She needed someone to talk this out with.

She paused at a red stoplight, thinking back at all the suspects they'd interviewed. Kirk Donovan. Peter Willington. Brendan Crenshaw. Frederick. Who else?

In her FBI training, she'd always been taught to go back to the last person who'd seen them alive.

With Marlene, that was Rick Loos. And he was out, because he was dead.

With Carlina, it was Evvie, and Brendan.

With Evvie, it was Brendan.

That seemed to suggest Brendan had something to do with it, and yet . . . he was with other people during Marlene's and Carlina's murders.

Her FBI training would say to look to where the victims were headed.

With Marlene, that was home. Or was she headed somewhere else?

With Carlina, that was back to Evvie's, and later, to meet up with Kirk Donovan.

A car behind her beeped. She realized the light had turned green and pumped on the gas, lurching forward.

She shook her head. This was pointless. They'd gone over everything before. Still, her mind couldn't stop spiraling.

With Evvie . . . she'd been on her way to see Fiona Prescott, the guidance counselor.

Was that strange? That they'd become friends even after school had ended?

Not too strange, she assumed. But what was interesting was that Mrs. Prescott had probably also been the guidance counselor of Carlina and Marlene.

And maybe they had told her secrets, too . . . secrets of things that had happened during school.

Was that possible?

Yes, but if Marlene had told Fiona in confidence about her relationship with Kirk Donovan, she'd be required to report it to authorities under mandatory reporting laws of child abuse. Wouldn't she?

Unless . . .

Mia swallowed as something came to her.

Unless Fiona Prescott, who had a relationship with Kirk Donovan as well, couldn't take that this girl was moving in on her man and murdered her out of jealousy.

She jammed on the brakes, skidding to the side of the road, tires squealing. Picking up her phone, she punched in *Fiona Prescott, Dallas.*

This time, a single address came up: 86 Spike Hollow Lane.

She made a quick U turn and headed toward the address. She had to see if her hunch was right.

CHAPTER TWENTY EIGHT

Fiona Prescott lived at a house that was almost an exact replica of Kirk Donovan's. Modest and unassuming, it lacked any landscaping or pride in ownership—it was simply a small box with tiny windows and no personality. Apparently, Fiona Prescott wasn't much of a Martha Stewart type.

Every room in the house was lit up. She climbed the steps to the door and peered in the half-open window, into a similarly bare living room with nothing but a couch and large-screen television set, affixed to the wall. No one was there, though *The Terminator* was playing on the screen. Canned gunshots emanated from the set.

Something crossed past the window on the other side of the staircase, which drew her attention there. Though it was half-obscured by some gauzy curtains, she noticed the slim form of a young woman who couldn't have been more than mid-twenties, moving like a tornado around the small, similarly unadorned bedroom, throwing clothes into the suitcase open on her king bed.

She looked like she was trying to make an escape. To run away from the bad things she'd done.

And that, to Mia, was suspicious enough.

She paused with her finger over the doorbell, considering. The woman looked so jumpy, she might try to run out a back door if she knocked. No. It was better to go with the element of surprise.

The porch extended far enough that she could easily stand by the window. Looking up and down the street, she made sure no one was watching. Then, she reached around the frame of the window and dislodged the screen, sliding it to the ground. Slowly pushing up the window with the heels of her hands so it wouldn't make too much noise, she lifted herself up on the ledge and pulled herself inside.

When she looked around, she noticed another suitcase by the door, packed and ready to go.

Mia was just crossing toward the bedroom door when the woman appeared. Her eyes went wide and she gasped. "What are you—"

"Fiona Prescott?"

She fumbled in the pockets of her jeans. The girl was slim and pretty, with long dark hair, pinned back with a clamshell clip at the crown of her head. She was wearing a tight, button-down shirt, the first few buttons open to reveal a heart-shaped locket. "What are you doing in my house? I'm calling the pol—"

"I don't think you will," Mia said evenly. "I think the police are the last people you want to see tonight. Considering you're trying to run away from them."

"What?" She hesitated, then put the phone back in her pocket. "I want you to leave."

Mia crossed her arms, rooting herself to the spot in the doorway. "Not until you admit what you've done."

She shook her head and started to walk to the door. "I don't admit to anything."

"So you weren't in a relationship with Kirk Donovan?"

She stopped and turned, running her eye over Mia. "Who are you? Police? FBI?"

"Neither. I'm just a concerned citizen. I know that you did it. I know that you killed Marlene Dotts, Carlina Adams, and Evelyn Rhinehart. I just want to know why." She took a step forward. "Was it because of Kirk?"

Mia though Fiona would try to deny it, but she simply nodded, very slowly at first, then with more authority. She seemed happy to get it out. "Kirk and I are going to go away together. Leave this place for good."

"Does he know that?"

She sighed, "He will. Once he realizes what I've done for him, he'll agree. He loves me. He just . . . he gets easily distracted. That's not his fault. It's those girls." She spat the last word with venom.

"How did you find out Marlene was having an affair with Kirk?"

She scoffed. "An anonymous note was sent to the guidance office, saying that one of us should look into it. I knew it was from Carlina, right away. She's not very bright, and she's always been a little schemer, jealous of Marlene. Marlene was beautiful, and had everything going for her. But when she tried to take Kirk away from me . . . I had it."

"You and Kirk—"

"We were in love. Yes. He didn't want to tell anyone because he thought it would affect our working relationship. But from the moment

I got there—two years ago—we've been together. And it was amazing." Her wistful expression gave way to an ugly scowl. "And then he met Marlene."

The look on Fiona's face was so jarring, so frightening, that Mia instinctively looked around for an escape. There wasn't one. Not that it mattered. Fiona was only a little thing. Mia could easily overpower her if she decided to attack. She wasn't worried. Not yet. "Did he try to break things off with you?"

She shook her head. "I went to his house and peeked in the window. Found them in bed together. And I saw red." She gritted her teeth. "I followed her, that afternoon. Watched her at soccer practice. Saw her having a fight with Loos, because that creepy guy always had a thing for his girls, especially Marlene. I knew that if I killed her, it'd be blamed on him. Then I caught up with her while she was walking home. I told her I knew about Kirk and said that I would tell the administration. She begged me not to."

"And then . . ."

"And then she told me that once she graduated, Kirk wanted to marry her." She rolled her eyes to the ceiling. "And I lost it. So I shoved her into the woods and we started fighting. She had a cord on her gym shorts. I managed to get it out and . . . that's it."

Mia swallowed. With that confession, the woman's eyes glinted with madness. She couldn't put it past her not to try the same thing with her. She needed to keep her talking, so she said, "And Carlina?"

"That bitch," she muttered with sigh. "I should've known that she would've made a play for Kirk after Marlene was dead. She always wanted everything Marlene had. But I didn't find out about it until a couple weeks ago, when I was in Kirk's classroom at school. He'd left his phone unattended and I found a text conversation he was having with her. He wanted to meet up with her. It was then I realized that she'd done the same thing Marlene did, and now he was screwing her, too."

"So that night . . ."

"I was waiting in her backyard, for her to come home. That was easy. Once you've killed one time, all the other ones are so easy."

Mia's mouth opened as the woman stood before her, shaking in rage. She took a step backwards, trying to process this admission, and the self-satisfied way in which she related the details. "And Evelyn?"

"Evvie was unfortunate," she said, showing what might have been real remorse. "She and I had always been very friendly, and she'd never mentioned anything to me about Kirk, so I assumed she had no idea. But then, when Carlina was murdered, she called me and wanted to meet. She said she thought it had to do with this secret lover of hers. It was then that I realized she probably knew. That Carlina had told her everything. And I couldn't have that."

"So you killed her, too?"

She shrugged. It was all so nonchalant.

And at that moment, Mia knew that Fiona wouldn't hesitate to do the same to her.

Mia let out a breath and reached into her pocket, trying to find the numbers to call David. "She didn't know. She wanted to meet with you as a friend. Because her best friend had been killed and she wanted someone to talk to."

Fiona's eyebrow went up. "Oh. Well, that's too bad then."

She pressed the send button to connect the call, hoping she had the right number. It began to buzz lightly against her thigh. "So your plan is to skip town, then? With Kirk?"

"Yep." She smiled dreamily. "I just booked our plane tickets. But I don't think I'll be telling you where we're headed. Not that you'll be telling anyone, anything, after today."

"Sorry to disappoint you, Fiona," she said, though she wasn't sorry in the least. "But Kirk's been arrested. They arrested him for the murders you committed. So you're going to have to take that flight alone."

A scowl fell upon her face. "You're lying."

"Nope. I just came from his place. They arrested him and he's going to go to jail for a long time. He doesn't have any alibi for those murders you committed. So if you love him and want him to go free, I think you have a decision to make."

She let out a cry of frustration.

"How stupid can they be! Like Kirk could ever harm anyone!" Her scowl deepened. "Who are you again? How do you know this?"

In her pocket, there was a click as the phone connected. Then a loud voice said, "Hunter, here."

Fiona's eyes filled with rage.

Shit, Mia thought. *She can hear it.*

“Who are you calling?” Fiona demanded, advancing as David Hunter’s voice continued to ask *Hello? Hello*? in her pocket. “Give me that phone right now!”

CHAPTER TWENTY NINE

Mia watched as Fiona pulled the pocket-knife from behind her back and waved it so that the metal shimmered in the lights above.

It occurred to Mia at that moment that she was hopelessly unarmed. She'd thought that she could bring down a little thing like Fiona with no trouble. But she hadn't factored in the knife. Instinctively, Mia took a step back. "Wait. Fiona. Put that away."

In her pocket, the phone had gone silent. She wasn't sure, now, if David was listening, or if he'd hung up, thinking it was a crank call.

"Why?" Fiona straightened, her features contorting. "God, you sound just like all of them."

Mia swallowed. "Like who?"

Her voice was a whisper. "All of those girls. Begging for their lives." She grinned and wiped the perspiration from her forehead with the back of her hand as she inspected the blade. "I kind of love the sound of it. I'll try a knife this time. I've always wanted to know what it feels like to dig a blade into a person. To *carve*."

Her eyes sparkled. Mia had no doubt that she was excited to use it. She held out her hand, palm up.

"Give me the phone."

Slowly, Mia reached into her pocket and pulled out her burner phone. Sure enough, the display was blank. The call had been disconnected.

Her last hope.

She swallowed and tried to back away, but in the last instant, Fiona threw the phone on the ground and as it skittered under a couch, jabbed the knife in her direction. Mia saw the point of the blade coming toward her and tried to block Fiona's hand, but while she managed to, she didn't notice her other hand, coming seemingly out of nowhere. It slammed against the side of her face, making her see stars.

Then, Fiona grabbed ahold of her wrist, wrenching her toward the ground. As she went stumbling, Fiona came up behind her, put a foot on her back, and pushed her flat on her stomach, to the wood floor.

All the air left Mia's lungs in a rush and her chin slammed against the hard surface, sending pain ricocheting through her skull.

Then she felt Fiona on her. She came behind Mia, grabbing her by the hair and lifting her back. "I don't know who you think you are, but guess what, bitch?" she snarled into her ear. "I'm a black belt in karate. Don't mess with me."

She took the blade and brought it against Mia's throat.

Mia's chest heaved. She gasped for breath. "Wait . . . no, wait . . ."

"Ready to die?" she whispered, exhaling slowly. "Don't worry, it'll all be over soon."

Mia whimpered, feeling the hot blade sting her skin.

She grabbed Mia by the hair and yanked her head back. A veil of hair covered her eyes. She could smell the scent of the woman's sweat, and the hand that pressed against her forehead was hot and moist. "Please…."

Mia felt the metal prick her skin and a burning, wet sensation, her skin opening up like a zipper. *This is it. The end.*

A crackling noise echoed behind her, very close at hand. Blade at the ready, Fiona turned her head in its direction and stood motionless.

It was the distraction she needed.

Taking a deep breath, she exploded with every bit of energy she had left in her, pinwheeling her arms and jarring her head back as hard as she could. Fiona let out a gasp and the grip upon Mia immediately loosened. There was the sound of breaking glass as a lamp fell to the ground, the bulb and its ceramic base shattering. Behind her, Fiona groaned, and she could hear the sound of the knife, skittering along the wood. Mia kicked up to her hands and knees and scurried away, as fast as she could, scanning the area for the dropped weapon.

Mia didn't know where to run to, where to escape. She propelled herself through the first open doorway, to the bedroom, grabbing the first thing she could. The lamp. The second she wrenched the cord from the outlet, everything went dark.

Fumbling in the sudden blackness, the backs of her knees hit the king bed. She skirted around it, her eyes adjusting just enough to see the form filling the doorway.

"Where are you, bitch?" she shouted, frantic. "I'm going to kill you."

Mia backed away, feeling a sudden wetness, seeping down the front of her shirt. With one hand, she reached up and found the stinging cut of the knife, about an inch long. Not too deep, she hoped, but the amount of blood soaking her skin was alarming.

Fiona's eyes must've been adjusting, too, because she seemed to walk straight toward Mia, standing in the remote corner. As she came closer, she stepped into a slice of moonlight. The blade in her hand glinted.

She'd recovered the blade.

When she was almost on top of her, Mia swung the lamp at her. It broke apart in her hands, leaving her weaponless, but it had one good effect—it pushed Fiona back long enough for Mia to escape.

She rocketed forward and threw herself over the bed, climbing madly over it on hands and knees and crashing to the ground on the other side. Then she began to run into the dark, a rat in a maze. She found the front door, but then she was upon her, on her back, pushing her with such force that at once, her knees buckled under the weight and she came crashing down. This time, her forehead and cheek grated against the hard floor, the metallic taste of blood soaked into her mouth. Fiona shoved her skull down so hard that Mia thought, for one mad, delirious second, it would be crushed.

Somehow—she didn't know how—she managed to wriggle enough to roll over, hair matted to her face and sticky with her own blood. Grasping blindly, she circled a hand around the wrist of the hand clasping the knife. Above her, Fiona's face was twisted in a mask of hatred and desperation. With her other hand, Mia plugged at her tiny fingers, ripping at each one, finally prying it from her grasp. It clattered to the floor near Mia's ear.

"I'm going to destroy you, bitch!" the woman snarled, wrapping her hands around Mia's neck.

Already out of breath, with the weight of the woman on her chest, the last bit of air was sucked almost immediately from Mia's lungs, and they began to burn. Mia fumbled for the knife, feeling nothing but her bloody hair. Finally, as the pain screamed inside her, she found the hilt of the knife. With all her strength, she lurched forward and dug it into Fiona's leg.

She yelped and growled in pain, like a wounded animal, and stumbled back.

Mia backed away on her hands and backside, trying to find the balance to get to her feet, but instead, she encountered another something hard. But this was not the knife; it was much larger. But just as lethal. As she took it in her hands, she knew exactly what it was.

The bottom weight from the broken lamp.

Mia couldn't see the girl coming toward her, but she could feel her getting nearer. And though she was ready to collapse from exhaustion, she knew she had the strength for this. When Fiona advanced again, she brought the weight down, as hard as she could, on the girl's head.

There was no sound. She simply collapsed, like dead weight, and did not move again.

Then, she collapsed to the floor once again.

Peace. With one eye, she spied the girl's body, still, on the floor, black blood glistening in the moonlight streaming through the window. She reached over and checked her pulse. Still alive.

When she had finally caught her breath, she thought she heard sirens in the distance. Good old David. She slid toward the couch, groping underneath it until she found her phone. She touched the display. Thank goodness. It still worked.

She pulled herself to her feet, threw herself toward the front door, limping, and disappeared into the night.

*

"Give me that phone right now!"

Or something like that.

That was all David Hunter had heard.

It was a female voice, but one he didn't know at all. What he did know, was the sound of the gasp that had followed. He'd been partners long enough with her, and they'd been in enough bad scrapes, for him to be intimately acquainted with that sound.

That was Mia.

And she was in trouble.

They'd been sitting in a conference room, across from Kirk Donovan. Kirk, the weakling, was blubbering about how Physics was his life and he couldn't imagine not being a teacher anymore. Then, as he wailed, "She attacked me! I thought she was going to kill me!" two things happened.

One: He realized that Mia had gotten to Kirk's house, first.

And two: His cell phone began to ring with a call from Mia's burner.

"Who's she?" he'd asked, standing up, wondering why Mia was calling him, now that the case was solved. The only reason she'd call him, now, would be . . . *if they arrested the wrong guy.*

And the guy in front of him, despite all signs pointing to him being the killer, didn't exactly seem like a murderer. He was sad, weak, and couldn't seem to string two words together when put under pressure. He blubbered, "I don't know! I never saw her before in my life."

He'd held up a finger to the other officers and the U.S. Marshal in the room. "I've got to take this."

Then he'd stepped outside the interrogation room and answered, only to hear those muffled words.

And it had all come together.

Another female had committed the murders—not a male, as they'd originally thought. Someone connected to all three girls, and to Kirk Donovan. After all, Carlina had been having an affair with him, and it stood to reason that someone had been jealous. But who? As he stood there, thinking, a bit of a conversation he'd had with Mia about Evelyn Rhinehart struck him:

"Yeah. From her texts, we know where she was headed. To a place called Rafferty's, downtown. It looks like she was meeting with a Fiona Prescott. She's a guidance counselor at the high school."

"But she graduated last year. Why would—"

"I know. She and Evelyn met up a lot. I guess they remained friends after graduation."

Of course. As a guidance counselor, she had access to all the girls. And as an employee of the school, she probably knew Kirk Donavan, too.

He'd burst into the room just as the U.S. Marshal was asking a question, and spoke over him. "Donovan, what do you know about Fiona Prescott?"

They'd all stared at him, shocked. Finally, Donovan had admitted what he'd been suspecting. "She's a guidance counselor at the school. We've dated a few times, but nothing serious."

He'd motioned to the Marshal to stand up. "I'm willing to bet she thought it was pretty serious," he'd said, rushing outside, ordering one of the police officers to find him the address of this guidance counselor.

Now, sitting outside the darkened house, he wondered if he was wrong.

"What's got us running out here like a bat out of hell?" Kane Wilcox said from the passenger seat, studying the place. "Looks empty."

He put his hand on the door handle. "You and I both know that the guy we have down at the station isn't capable of strangling three women."

Wilcox glanced at him. "Do we?"

David got it. He was testing him, trying to see if he'd gotten his information from an outside source, namely, Mia.

If she was here, she'd be arrested, too.

But during that call, she'd been in trouble. Better to be alive and in prison, than dead. He pushed open the door. "Yeah. This woman's a guidance counselor at the school. And like Kirk said, they were romantically involved. I think she killed the girls out of jealousy because of their relationships with him."

He jogged up to the front door and knocked. "FBI. Open up."

No answer. He waited only a second before trying the doorknob. It was open.

He pushed open the door and felt around for a light switch. When he found it and the room was filled with light, the first thing he saw was the blood. There were bits of broken ceramic and splintered furniture, too.

"Hell," Wilcox said behind him, as he reached for his gun. Holding it at the ready, he inched forward, back against the wall, then swung into the living room.

In the darkened room, David could see a woman, lying on her back among the rubble. There was a heavy purple bruise on her forehead, bleeding. She moaned slightly.

That had to have been Fiona Prescott.

He glanced around. No Mia.

But she'd been here, all right, and made an impression. He let out a sigh of relief and knelt over the woman. "Fiona Prescott?" he asked as her eyes fluttered open.

She let out another long moan in answer.

"You're under arrest," he said, as Wilcox moved about the place, turning on lights, looking for someone else.

"What the hell happened here?" He asked, gritting his teeth. "How'd she get like that?"

"Don't know," David said, not looking up.

"Bullshit," he grumbled. "You know."

David Hunter raised his head and met his eyes. "Anything I could tell you would just be a guess. All I can tell you, Agent, is that it looks like someone else solved this case, first."

Wilcox's eyes narrowed. "North?"

Hunter shrugged. "Like I said, I haven't spoken to her. So I can't speculate."

Wilcox turned around, grumbling curses, and punched his fist into the wall. Behind him, Hunter couldn't help but smile.

CHAPTER THIRTY

Back in University Park, in the early hours of morning, Mia sat a few houses away from her home and finished tending to her wounds. She'd gotten some wet paper towels from a public restroom and used it to clean up the bloody wound at her throat, and with a little pressure, the flow seemed to be subsiding. Other than that, a few bruises and sprains, but she'd be okay.

Right now, she just needed to go somewhere and rest up.

But her home was on the way out of town, and she couldn't resist stopping there, for just one more look.

Kelsey was likely asleep. Aiden, however, had told her he wasn't sleeping much with her gone. She wondered if he was awake, thinking about her.

She couldn't take chances, like she had before. Things were getting far more dangerous. And with Kane Wilcox on her tail—well, he didn't look like an idiot. She'd have to be far more careful, going forward.

Which meant that stopping here, on this street, this place she used to call her refuge from all the bad that she dealt with in her day-to-day job, was now off-limits.

As she was sitting there, preparing to drive off, her phone buzzed with a text. From David.

Got her. Thanks for your help. We never would've put it together without you.

She smiled. At least someone appreciated her. And right now, it was the least she could do. The *only* thing she could do. She was born for this job—solving cold cases. And maybe being a criminal, she could go against the rules and do things a little better.

She typed in: *And the marshal?*

A moment later, he responded with: *Hot on your tail. He knows it was you. Be careful.*

As always, she thought, and typed in: *You think you can get me a gun?*

It was a tall order, she knew. One that could get him in a lot of trouble. But if she'd faced down Fiona with a gun, the game would've changed. A gun would've changed everything. She felt naked without one. And Hunter could easily secure an unmarked one that could never be traced to him. He had access to the gun depository at headquarters, which was full of old guns, most of which no one would ever miss.

But Hunter was a good guy. He played by the rules. Even just communicating with her was against his credo.

She expected a flat-out refusal, but he simply said, *I'll see what I can do.*

She smiled.

Lay low, he texted her then. *I'll be in touch.*

She would try. She knew he was a man of his word, but she couldn't make any promises. She was never one who liked to wait.

Opening up her search app, she typed in: *Wilson Andrews.*

The first article to come up? *Wilson Andrews Gearing up for campaign event in University Park.*

Well, wasn't that serendipitous. It was at the Hyatt, practically around the block from where her car idled.

She opened up her messages and typed in a text to her partner: *You know me.*

His response came in a moment later: *That's what I'm afraid of.*

*

Twenty minutes later, Mia sat in the parking lot of the Hyatt, watching and waiting.

Knowing Wilson Andrews, he likely had the penthouse suite.

Knowing him, he wasn't alone. He likely had several mistresses—that was the rumor—but he also had an entourage of bodyguards. He needed them, considering how many people he'd wronged in his lifetime.

It was infuriating that, considering his life of cheating and swindling, of lying to protect his serial-killer brother, of dodging underneath the snares of dozens of eye-opening scandals, he still managed to be ahead in the polls.

This November, if what the political pundits were saying was true, he'd be elected by a landslide. Any bad press seemed to bounce off him, like he was wearing a suit of armor.

Maybe it was a good thing David hadn't given her a gun yet.

Because she felt just crazy enough, right now, to use it on him. If only she could get close enough.

Pulling her hood tight over her head, she stepped out of her car and walked to the service entrance of the hotel. There was no one in sight. She stepped through the heavy door, expecting someone to stop her, but nobody did. Then, she walked down a long hallway, coming to a service elevator.

I wonder if this goes up to the penthouse? I bet that scumbag's asleep in his bed right now. If I had a gun, I could just take the elevator up, fire the gun, and be gone before his thugs were the wiser.

But that wouldn't help. That would only make her more guilty. She couldn't incriminate herself. As much as she wanted revenge on him, she wanted to be back with her family, too. And so that meant she needed to find overwhelming evidence that would finally, once and for all, prove that she was innocent.

As she was backing away, the elevator dinged, and the doors slowly began to open.

She ducked into the laundry room, hiding behind an industrial-sized, wheeled laundry bin, and peered out.

It was Wilson Andrews. He was in dark sweats, a hat pulled down over his face, but she'd been studying his picture so much over the last few months, she knew him well. She watched as he strode toward the exit and stood there, at the door, waiting.

Like this, in black, he was the exact opposite of the man he presented to the world—that baby-kissing, waving, smiling representative of the American Dream.

That meant he was up to no good. *What are you up to, you snake?*

She watched closely, waiting for him to make a move.

Within moment, a short, stocky man approached, wearing a thick coat, too warm for the night, pulled up to his ears. He had a skull cap pulled down low over his head.

"What the hell? You have a lot of nerve, keeping me waiting," Andrews said in a low voice.

"Yo, I'm sorry, I'm sorry," the man said with a shrug. "My car wouldn't start."

"You think I give a shit?" Andrews snapped. "You understand what needs to happen?"

"Yeah. Yeah. No sweat," the man said, his voice jumpy. "I got it."

"Good." She watched as Andrews reached into the pocket of his sweatshirt and pulled out a thick envelope. Probably full of money. Mia couldn't see the money, but she knew a shady deal when she saw one.

This was a hit. Was this the same guy who'd killed Ellis Horvath? Maybe Reynolds hadn't been the person there, or maybe there'd been a few people in the warehouse, that night she was set up. The questions teemed in her mind as she watched Wilson Andrews head back to the elevator.

His back was to her.

Her hands tightened into fists. If she wanted to, she could easily jump out. Overpower him. And end him, right here. Every pore within her screamed for her to do it, to seek out the justice she deserved and make him feel the pain she'd been suffering with, for the past months.

But then she'd never see Aiden or Kelsey again. That was certain.

The elevator doors opened, and she watched him step inside. He pressed a button, jabbing it impatiently, and then the doors closed, and he was gone.

She was alone.

Aching, she limped to the door and went back to her car. As she slid behind the wheel, she thought about the dirty deal she'd just witnessed.

Whatever Wilson Andrews was paying the thug for, it wasn't anything good, and would probably destroy a person's life. Just like hers.

So who was the lucky winner?

CHAPTER THIRTY ONE

It'd be easy enough to get the gun Mia wanted.

David Hunter knew this. There were hundreds of unmarked guns in the depository. Any agent could go in and help himself.

But agents were sworn to a code of ethics. And it was that code of ethics they were held to. The FBI trusted him not to screw around.

And until Mia North had escaped from prison, he'd trusted himself, too.

Now, David wasn't sure. He could help her. So easily.

He waved at a couple of people in the hallway. To them, it was just another day. But as David took the elevator to the basement, something that they likely didn't notice was the war being waged in David's head.

Should I? Shouldn't I?

Hadn't he just had this conversation with Louie, who'd taken two pieces of candy from the preacher's candy basket after mass on Sunday morning? Louie had shrugged and said, "Dad, it doesn't matter. Father Ibsen doesn't have them counted."

David had looked at his son and shaken his head. "Just because you can get away with a thing, doesn't mean you should. Right is right."

Right was right.

And right now, he was definitely wrong. Even though he'd redeemed himself to Louie, attending the last two of his baseball games, including the one where he batted in the game-winning run, David felt like a big hypocrite, a liar, a failure to his son.

Yet something kept him walking down the hall to the storage lockers.

Two seconds. That's all it took. He went in, made sure the cameras weren't facing his way, took the key off the wall, grabbed a Baretta 9mm from one of the lockers, stuffed it into his empty shoulder holster, and voila.

Done.

Candy, taken from that baby.

With every step he took away from that storage room, though, he felt worse and worse. It was hanging over him like a specter by the time he reached his desk. He'd just bent over his desk, and was about to stick the gun in his briefcase, when a voice behind him said, "Hunter."

He turned to face the imposing form of U.S. Marshal Kane Wilcox.

"Yes?" he said, his voice wobbling.

The Marshal strode confidently into his cubicle, sat down across from his desk, and put his feet up on it. The jerk had been slowly weaseling his way into the Dallas Fort Worth police force, and what was even more unbelievable was that Lieutenant Briggs, who seemed to have an aversion to all Feds, had actually let him.

"So. I thought you and I could catch up."

David Hunter's pulse pounded under his collar. He glanced at his open briefcase, and re-buttoned his blazer. "About what?"

"That last case was pretty wild, huh? Any loose ends?"

He shook his head and went to his chair. "No."

"You sure?"

He gritted his teeth and leveled his gaze at the Marshal. "I don't know what you're getting at."

"Well, I still think back to that night. How your prime suspect was laid out for you, so nicely like that. Whoever did it might as well have left you a greeting card."

Hunter lowered his gaze to his blotter. "And?"

"And," he said, leaning forward and smirking. "I think you know who did it."

He shrugged. "I think you're wrong."

"That's funny. Because I just got back from the lab and it's like I thought. Your partner's fingerprints and blood samples are all over that house. On the knife. On the floor. On the suspect. Everywhere."

He froze. They'd gotten their woman, and she'd confessed. Prescott, once she'd come to, had folded like a house of cards, admitting to committing all of the murders, out of jealousy, because she couldn't bear to see Kirk Donovan with anyone else. Open and shut case. No need for lab tests. "I didn't order any—"

"Yeah. I did." His smile widened.

"Last I checked, this wasn't your case. What authorization do you have to—"

"Believe me, it's all in order."

Somehow, he'd been anticipating this. He'd seen the way the Marshal had stalked about the place. He'd watched him crouch in front of the blood, staring at it with great interest. He should've known he'd have collected those samples.

"Fine. Well," he began, ready to tell him he had no idea what it meant. "Like I said, I never—"

He slammed his fists down on the desk. "You knew Mia was there because she called you. When we were in the interrogation room with Donovan, you received a phone call. From her. Admit it."

He sucked in a breath. "I'll admit no such thing. Can you please leave my—"

"No, Hunter."

He looked up. His boss, Special Agent in Charge Pembroke, was standing in the doorway. He stepped in and closed the door. David Hunter's stomach dropped.

"I think this is something you need to answer for, Agent," Pembroke said, crossing his arms. "Are you helping Mia North?"

He stood there, both answers, yes and no, hovering on his lips. He could tell the truth, and get into some trouble. Maybe lose his job. Lie, and down the road, he'd end up in prison. Every option sucked.

So he said nothing.

Agent Pembroke leaned in more. "Answer, me, Agent. If there's anything you want to tell us, now is the time."

NOW AVAILABLE!

<u>SEE HER SCREAM</u>
(A Mia North FBI Suspense Thriller—Book 3)

Fugitive FBI Agent Mia North rushes to a commune in the Southwestern desert, where bodies are turning up murdered in ritualistic ways. Can she find and stop the killer—and figure out who framed her—before she is caught by the U.S. Marshals?

In SEE HER RUN (A Mia North FBI Suspense Thriller—Book One), Special Agent Mia North is a rising star in the FBI—until, in an elaborate setup, she's framed for murder and sentenced to prison. When a lucky break allows her to escape, Mia finds herself a fugitive, on the run and on the wrong side of the law for the first time in her life. She can't see her young daughter—and she has no hope of returning to her former life.

The only way to get her life back, she realizes, is to hunt down whoever framed her.

Mia, still on the run, is summoned by her ex-partner when a new apparent serial killer surfaces. The new case will lead her, working in the shadows, to a creepy commune in the Southwest, where red herrings abound. Mia knows her only hope of getting answers is to infiltrate the commune—but its members aren't exactly welcoming.

Worse, Mia is desperate to contact her daughter, but the U.S. Marshals are getting closer.

As she turns up a shocking revelation and inches close to figuring out who framed her, the noose is closing in.

Can Mia solve the case in time to escape herself?

An action-packed page-turner, the MIA NORTH series is a riveting crime thriller, jammed with suspense, surprises, and twists and turns that you won't see coming. Fall in love with this brilliant new female protagonist and you'll be turning pages late into the night.

Future books in this series will be available soon!

Rylie Dark

Debut author Rylie Dark is author of the SADIE PRICE FBI SUSPENSE THRILLER series, comprising six books (and counting); the MIA NORTH FBI SUSPENSE THRILLER series, comprising three books (and counting); the CARLY SEE FBI SUSPENSE THRILLER, comprising three books (and counting); and the MORGAN STARK FBI SUSPENSE THRILLER, comprising three books (and counting).

An avid reader and lifelong fan of the mystery and thriller genres, Rylie loves to hear from you, so please feel free to visit www.ryliedark.com to learn more and stay in touch.

BOOKS BY RYLIE DARK

SADIE PRICE FBI SUSPENSE THRILLER
ONLY MURDER (Book #1)
ONLY RAGE (Book #2)
ONLY HIS (Book #3)
ONLY ONCE (Book #4)
ONLY SPITE (Book #5)
ONLY MADNESS (Book #6)

MIA NORTH FBI SUSPENSE THRILLER
SEE HER RUN (Book #1)
SEE HER HIDE (Book #2)
SEE HER SCREAM (Book #3)

CARLY SEE FBI SUSPENSE THRILLER
NO WAY OUT (Book #1)
NO WAY BACK (Book #2)
NO WAY HOME (Book #3)

MORGAN STARK FBI SUSPENSE THRILLER
TOO LATE (Book #1)
TOO CLOSE (Book #2)
TOO FAR GONE (Book #3)

www.ingramcontent.com/pod-product-compliance
Lightning Source LLC
Chambersburg PA
CBHW030615310726
48979CB00003B/724

* 9 7 8 1 0 9 4 3 9 3 8 3 4 *